I0831484

S. Hall Young

Adventures in Alaska

Outlook

S. Hall Young

Adventures in Alaska

1. Auflage | ISBN: 978-3-73262-049-4

Erscheinungsort: Frankfurt am Main, Deutschland

Erscheinungsjahr: 2018

Outlook Verlag GmbH, Frankfurt.

S. Hall Young

Adventures in Alaska

Outlook

Adventures in Alaska

By

S. HALL YOUNG

Author of "Alaska Days with John Muir,"

"The Klondike Clan"

ILLUSTRATED

NEW YORK CHICAGO

Fleming H. Revell Company

LONDON AND EDINBURGH

FLEMING H. REVELL COMPANY
New York: 158 Fifth Avenue
Chicago: 17 North Wabash Ave.
London: 21 Paternoster Square
Edinburgh: 75 Princes Street

Stalking Walrus in an Oomiak

Dr. Young's figure is to the left. This is the time he got his ivory for the gavels

Foreword

THE author puts forth this little book of actual adventures in the great new land of Alaska with the hope that it will afford healthy-minded young people a true idea of some phases of human and animal life there. These stories are picked out of an experience of forty years and selected with a view to both unity and variety.

The first three chapters are an attempt to draw in bold outline some dramatic episodes of the author's experience in the second of the three great gold stampedes of the Northwest. All these struggles for gold have in them richly dramatic elements. Life in such camps pulses strongly with all human ambitions, affections and passions. The missionary, if he is really to commend himself to the men who rush into the wilderness for gold, and do them good, must, first of all, prove himself a *man*, ready and able to do and suffer everything that falls to the lot of the gold seekers. He must live their life and play the game with them. He must cheerfully put up with the privations they endure, must take the lead in their healthy sports, must alleviate their sufferings, and, keeping himself free from the deadly gold-lust, must show that he has in himself and can give to his fellow pioneers something better than gold. His heart must be, for himself and those about him, a living fountain of joy and peace.

As in his earlier work, "The Klondike Clan," the author endeavored to draw a true picture not only of the life and conditions of the first Northwestern gold-rush, but also of the minister's aims and field of duty; so in this short sketch of the second Stampede his aim has been, above all things, *truth*. Every incident is actual history, and even the names are real. The dog story is also conscientiously true history, and belongs to one of the minor gold stampedes.

The second section of the book—the three bear stories and the walrus story—are also bits of history. Every pioneer missionary in Alaska should be an ardent hunter. The author's life has often depended upon his gun and fishing tackle. For ten years in Southeastern Alaska he and his family had no beef or pork or mutton, but the game—animals, birds and fish—more than made up for the lack of these.

In Interior Alaska the same conditions prevail. The wild animals furnish not only the food of the people, both natives and whites, but also their winter clothing. Life would be unbearable there in "sixty-below weather" were the inhabitants unable to procure the warm coats provided by kindly Mother Nature for the use both of her four-footed and her human children.

The Eskimo faces the hardest conditions of almost any native race in his battle for life; and yet he is, perhaps, the most comfortable of any. He gets his living from the Arctic seas, the seal and walrus being his main dependence. From the great walrus he gets meat, clam chowder, light and fuel; its skin makes his foot-wear, the walls and roof of his house, and his boats; its ivory furnishes his tools and implements of the chase. When the author and his friends brought the great supply of walrus meat to the Eskimo village of East Cape they insured the life and comfort of its inhabitants for the winter. All this is an essential part of a missionary's beneficent work. Good service for God and humanity is not inconsistent with the joy of the chase.

As the author confidently expects that many of his young readers will find their permanent homes in "The great big, broad land 'way up yonder," he hopes this book may prove, in some degree, an introduction to the enjoyments and achievements of the life there.

S. H. Y.
New York.

CHAPTER I

THE NOME STAMPEDE

IT was with the excitement of a veteran soldier going into a fresh battle that I teetered over the springy plank from the Rampart shore to the deck of the Yukon River steamboat. My year's outfit of "grub and duds," as the miners would put it, was aboard. I grasped the hand of Dr. Koonce, with whom I had just floated in an open boat down the Yukon twelve hundred miles. A fine fellow—"Kooncie"! We had been camping, and fishing, and packing, and boating together since the first of May, 1899, and it was now the middle of August. He was to stay at the new mining town of Rampart, build a church there and learn the joyous life of a pioneer missionary.

What a queer mix-up of men on the crowded decks of the steamboat! Wild rumors of a ridiculous sort had reached the ears of gold hunters clear up the two thousand miles of the swift and crooked Yukon to Dawson. Gold! Not snugly reposing in the frozen gravel of deep gulches and canyons cut through the high hills—where respectable and orthodox gold ought to be; but gold on the wind-swept, stormy, treeless, exposed coast of Seward Peninsula—the tongue that impudent young Alaska sticks out at old Asia. Gold, like yellow corn-meal, in the beach-sands of Bering Sea, where nobody could lawfully stake a claim, but where anybody could go with shovel, pan and rocker and gather it up. Nuggets a-plenty and coarse gold—enticing shallow diggings—in the bed of Anvil Creek and other creeks and runlets in the hills, and the flat tundra about Nome.

The reports of the new "strike," often wild and exaggerated, came as a life-saver to weary and discouraged thousands of Klondikers, who had packed their outfits over the terrible thirty miles of the Chilcoot Pass in the fall of '97 or the spring of '98, sawed the lumber themselves in the "armstrong sawmill," sailed their clumsy boats through the lakes, shot the rapids of the Upper Yukon, spent the summer of '98 and the winter that followed surging here and there on "wildcat" stampedes or putting down "dry" holes on unprofitable lays, and were now eagerly snatching at this new straw, hoping to "strike it" on the Nome beach. From Dawson, Forty Mile, Eagle, Circle, Fort Yukon; from wood camps and prospectors' tents along the Yukon, and now from Rampart, these bearded, battered, sun-blistered men came rushing aboard the steamboat.

I had engaged a state-room before the steamboat arrived, but when it came a placard of the company owning the boat menaced us in the office: "*All reservations cancelled. Boat overcrowded. No passengers to be taken at Rampart.*"

Of course there was a mighty howl from the Rampart men, nearly half of whom had packed up to go on the boat. I hurried to the purser, whom I knew, and showed my pass from the manager of the company.

"Can't help it, Doctor," he said in a loud tone, for the benefit of the bystanders. "The boat's past her limit now, and we're liable for big damages if anything happens. We can't take *anybody*."

Presently he slyly pulled my arm, and I followed him to an inner office of the store. "Get your goods aboard," he directed. "You can spread your blankets on the floor of my office."

While I was checking off my outfit and seeing it on board, I noticed a lot of the Rampart men, with hand-trucks gathered from the various stores, taking their own outfits aboard, ignoring the shipping clerk and dumping their goods wherever they found a place to put them. The officers and deck-hands were protesting and swearing, but the men went right along loading their outfits.

Presently the captain pulled the whistle rope and ordered the plank drawn in and the cable cast off from the "dead man." Instantly three men marched to the cable's end, seized the man who was to cast it off and held him. Then fully fifty men with their packs on their backs filed down the plank. The first mate tried to stop them. He even made a move to draw his pistol; but the foremost man—a big six-footer—threw his arms around him and carried him back against the stairway and held him until the men with their packs were all aboard. It was all done quietly, and with the utmost good humor. The men grinned up at the swearing, red-faced captain on the upper deck, and one shouted, "We'll give you a poke of dust, Cap., when we get to Nome."

When all were aboard, somebody on the bank cast off the cable, the swift current caught the boat, the wheel backed, and we swung around and headed down the Yukon, bound for the new strike.

Whiskers were very much in evidence in that closely packed mob of men that stood around on all the decks, stepping on each other's feet, perching on stairways, boxes, pole-bunks—anywhere for a resting place. To go from one part of the boat to another was a difficult proposition.

The most evident trait of the crowd was its good nature. The deck-hands, among whom I recognized a lawyer friend from Dawson and a former customs collector from Juneau, were gold-seekers like all the rest; and it was, "Hello, Shorty!" "Ah, there, Dutch!" "Where you goin', Jim?" between them and the newcomers. A rollicking, happy-go-lucky crowd, all joyful at being on the way to the new diggings. Even the officers of the boat began to smile, secretly pleased that they had a record-breaking and most profitable load aboard, and were free from blame for overloading, because they could not help it.

As for me, I was well content, even to be hustled and jostled and elbow-punched by this horde of scraggly-bearded men of the northwestern wilderness. This was my parish, my home; and these were my comrades, my chums, my brothers. I was just as sunburned and weather-beaten as they were, and felt the same tingling of nerves, the same leap of the blood at the call of fresh adventure.

I was dressed in the same sort of rough woolen mackinaw clothes and soft flannel underwear as the men around me. I had left my clerical suit and white shirts and collars behind, for three reasons: First, for the sake of economy. These strong, loose garments did not cost a third as much as broadcloth, and would wear twice as well. Besides, it would cost a dollar and a half to have a white shirt laundered in Interior Alaska (which, at that time, was twice the original cost of the shirt), and twenty-five cents to do up a collar, the cost price of which "outside" was three for a quarter. I could wash my flannel shirts myself. Second, for comfort's sake. The soft wool of these garments was so much warmer and more pliable than a "Prince Albert" suit; and a starched collar would sear one's neck like fire, when it was "sixty below." My chief reason, however, was that I wished to create no artificial barriers between my parishioners and myself. I wished to stand on the same social level. I desired these men to feel that I was one of them, and could camp and "rustle," carry a pack, live on rabbits and rough it generally as deftly and cheerfully as they—live the same outdoor life and endure the same so-called "hardships."

The view-point of these "sour-doughs" was shown in a funny way at our first landing place after leaving Rampart, which was the little town of Tanana. When the boat tied up, the whistle gave three sharp hoots, showing that the stay would be very short. As soon as the plank was ashore a man ran up it, and when he reached the deck he called loudly: "Is there a preacher aboard? Is there a preacher aboard?"

A grizzled old miner, who did not know me, pointed to the only man on the steamboat who wore a Prince Albert coat and white shirt and collar, and drawled: "Wa-al, that there feller, he's either a preacher or a gambler; I don't know which."

The "dressed-up" man proved to be a gambler. I made myself known to the anxious man from the village, followed him ashore and married him to a woman who was waiting in the company's office.

That was one voyage of mingled discomfort and pleasure. Discomforts and hardships are as you make them and take them. There were a few of that company who grumbled and swore at being crowded, at being obliged to stand up all day, to lie on the floor or on the piles of cord-wood at night, besides being compelled to fairly fight for their meals or to get their food from their own kits. But the majority of these men had been camping and roughing it for two years. Many of them had packed heavy loads over the Chilcoot Pass in the great Klondike Stampede, had made their own boats and navigated hundreds of miles of unknown and dangerous rivers, had encountered and overcome thousands of untried experiences. To all of them these little discomforts were trifles to be dismissed with a smile or joke, and they had contempt for any man who fussed or complained.

One of the cheeriest of the crowd aboard the steamboat was a newsboy twelve or thirteen years old. His name was Joe: I never knew his surname. He had had a very wonderful time. The year before—the summer of 1898—he was selling papers in Seattle. He heard of the high prices paid for newspapers and magazines at the camps of the Northwest. He bought three or four hundred copies of the Seattle P. I. (*Post Intelligencer*) and *Times*. He paid two and a half and three cents apiece for them, the selling price at Seattle being five cents. Then he got five or six hundred back numbers of these papers, from a day to a week old, for nothing. He also got, mostly by gift from those who had read them, three or four hundred of the cheaper magazines, some new, some a month or two old. For his whole stock he paid scarcely fifteen dollars.

Joe smuggled himself and his papers aboard a steamboat bound for Skagway, and worked his passage as cabin boy, waiter and general roustabout. At Juneau and Skagway he sold about one-fourth of his papers and magazines— the papers for twenty-five cents each and the ten-cent magazines for fifty cents. He could have sold out, but hearing that he could get double these prices at Dawson and down the Yukon, held on to his stock.

He formed a partnership with an old "sour-dough" miner, who helped him get his papers over the Chilcoot Pass and down the Yukon to Dawson. At the great Klondike camp he quickly sold out his papers at a dollar each, and the magazines at a dollar and a half to two and a half.

Joe spent the winter of 1898-9 at Dawson, selling the two papers published in that city and running a general news stand, in which he sold the reading matter he had sold before but gathered up again from the buyers. Sometimes he sold the same magazine four or five times.

When the Nome Stampede began, Joe got into the good graces of the manager of the steamboat company and got free passage down the Yukon. He shared my wolf-robe on the floor of the purser's room, and we became great chums.

The boy was so bright and quick, and at the same time so polite and accommodating, that he made friends everywhere. He was a Sunday-school boy, and distributed my little red hymn-books when I held service in the social hall of the steamboat on Sunday, and his clear soprano sounded sweetly above the bass notes of the men.

"Joe," I asked him one day, "how much money have you made during the last year and a half?"

"Well," he replied, "I sent two thousand dollars out home from Dawson before I started down here, and with what I am making on this trip and what I hope to make at Nome, I think I'll have five thousand dollars clear when I land at Seattle the last of October."

"That's a dangerous amount of money for a small boy to have," I warned him. "Have you lost any of it?"

Joe grinned. "No, I dassen't. Some card sharps tried to get me to gamble at Dawson. They said I could double my money. But my partner [the old miner] said he'd lick me half to death if I ever went near the green tables. I didn't want to, anyhow. Everybody helps me take care of my money."

"What are you going to do with it?"

"Why, give it all to mother, of course. She'll use it for me and my sister. I'm going to school as soon as I get home. Mother works in a store, but I guess this money'll give her a rest. She needs it."

A word more about little Joe before I leave him. He made good at Nome in September, and sailed for Seattle the last of October. The last I heard of him, four or five years later, he was making his way through the University of Washington, and still managing newspaper routes in Seattle. His is a case of exceptional good fortune; and yet I know of a number of boys who have made remarkable sums selling papers in Alaska. It is a boy's land of opportunity as well as a man's.

Our voyage to St. Michael was a tedious one—down the long stretches of the Lower Yukon, worming through the sand-bars and muddy shallows of the interminable delta, waiting through weary hours for tide and wind to be just right before venturing out on Bering Sea. Hurrying at last under full steam through the choppy sea, with the waves washing the lower deck and producing panic, uproar and swearing among the men packed upon it—we came to the harbor of St. Michael on the wind-swept, treeless, mossy shore of Norton Sound.

I was still to work my way through a tangle of delays and adventures before I could reach my goal—the great new camp at Nome, one hundred and thirty miles from St. Michael.

I had first to get my outfit together on the wharf, counting the boxes and war bags, pursuing the missing ones to other outfits and proving my claim to them. In the confusion this was a hard job, but I only lost two or three of my boxes. I piled my goods in a corner of the big warehouse of the North American Trading and Transportation Co., and set up my tent on the beach, for I was near the end of my money, and could not pay the high prices charged at the hotels. I got into my camp kit and did my own cooking, protecting my food as best I could against the thievish Eskimo dogs.

Then began a search, which lasted a week, for means of getting to Nome. The gold-hunters were putting off every day in whale boats, Eskimo *oomiaks*, and small sloops and schooners; but these craft were too small and uncertain for me to risk passage in them. My caution proved wise, for five or six of these small boats, after setting out, were never heard of again.

While I was waiting, the U. S. Revenue Cutter, *Bear*, came into the harbor, and aboard her was Sheldon Jackson, Superintendent of Education for Alaska, the noted pioneer missionary. He was just returning from a tour of the native schools and reindeer stations. (He was the man who had introduced the reindeer into Alaska from Siberia to supply the wants of the Eskimo.)

"Hurry on to Nome," he counseled me. "You were never needed more in all your life."

At length there limped into the harbor a little tub-like side-wheel steamboat, belonging to the Alaska Exploration Company, whose wharf was a mile and a half distant up the harbor. There was no way of getting my goods across the swampy tundra of St. Michael Island to the wharf. On the beach I found an abandoned old rowboat with open seams. I procured pieces of boards, some oakum and pitch, and set to work to repair the old boat. The steamboat was to sail for Nome the next forenoon. I worked all night. I made a pair of clumsy oars out of boards. Then I carried my goods to the leaky boat and rowed them to the dock. It took three trips to transfer my outfit, and while I was rowing back and forth somebody carried off my most valuable war-bag, containing most of my foot-wear and underclothes—one hundred dollars' worth.

I was a tired man when I stumbled down the steep stairs into the dark and stuffy hold of the little steamboat; and much more tired when, after two and a half days of seasickness, bobbing up and down in the choppy seas like a man on a bucking broncho, I pulled up the stairs again and let myself down the rope-ladder into the dory which was to take the passengers ashore at Nome.

"You can only take what you can carry on your back," announced the captain. "There's a storm coming up and I've got to hurry to the lee of Sledge Island, twenty miles away. You'll get your outfits when I come back. Lucky we're not all down in Davy Jones's locker."

I strapped my pack-sack, containing my wolf-robe and a pair of blankets, on my back, glad to get ashore on any terms. The dory wallowed heavily in the waves, the strong wind driving it towards the sandy beach. Boats have to anchor from one to two miles offshore at Nome. When we reached the beach, a big wave lifted the dory and swung it sideways. The keel struck the sand, and she turned over, dumping us all out, the comber overwhelming us and rolling us over and over like barrels. Drenched and battered, we crawled to land.

A heavy rain was falling as I staggered up the beach with my water-soaked blankets on my back, looking for a lodging-house. The beach was lined with tents, placed without regard to order or the convenience of anybody except the owner of each tent. A few straggling board-shacks were stuck here and there on the swampy tundra. Two or three large, low store buildings represented the various pioneer trading companies. The one street, which ran parallel to the beach, was full of mud. The buildings most in evidence were saloons, generally with dance-hall attachments. The absence of trees, the leaden, weeping sky, the mud, the swampy tundra, the want of all light and beauty, made this reception the dreariest of all my experiences in the new mining camps.

Nome, Alaska, Summer of 1900

A city of tents, twenty miles long

But I long ago learned that nothing is so bad but that it might be worse. I had not at that time seen Edmund Vance Cook's sturdy lines, but the spirit of them was in my heart:

"Did you tackle the trouble that came your way
    With a resolute heart and cheerful,
Or hide your face from the light of day
    With a craven heart and fearful?
Oh, a trouble's a ton or a trouble's an ounce,
    Or a trouble is what you make it;
And it isn't the fact that you're hurt that counts,
    But only, how did you take it!"

I soon found a sign written in charcoal on the lid of a paper box—*Lodging*. I entered the rough building and found a cheery Irish woman named M'Grath. There was no furniture in the house except two or three cheap chairs and a home-made board table.

"Shure, ye can," she answered in reply to my question about spending the night there. "Ye'll spread yer robe an' blankets on the flure, an' it'll only cost ye a dollar an' four bits. Ye'll plaze pay in advance."

I took stock of the contents of my pocketbook. There was just five dollars and a quarter left of the thousand dollars with which I had started from home on the first of May. It was now the first of September, and no more money was due me until the next spring. My food and tent were on the steamboat and would not be likely to come ashore for many days. It was Sunday evening, and a whole week must elapse before I could take up a collection.

I paid my landlady and she put my blankets by her stove to dry. I paid another dollar and a half for a supper of beans and flap-jacks—the first food I had tasted for three days. I slept soundly that night on the floor, without a care or anxiety. The next morning I paid another dollar and a half for breakfast, and could not resist the temptation of purchasing a Seattle paper (only three weeks old—what a luxury!). I had just twenty-five cents left—and I was a stranger in this strange corner of the earth!

I could not help laughing at my predicament as I entered the Alaska Exploration Company's store. A bearded man standing by the stove bade me "good-morning."

"You seem to be pleased about something," he said. "Have you struck it rich?"

"Well, yes!" I replied; "a rich joke on me," and I told him of the fix I was in.

"What? You are Dr. Young?" he exclaimed, shaking me heartily by the hand. "Why, I'm a Presbyterian elder from San Francisco."

The man's name was Fickus, a carpenter, who had come to Nome to build the store and warehouses of one of the big companies. He had held the first religious meetings in the new camp and had found quite a circle of Christian people.

He offered to lend me money, but I refused to take it. "No," I said, "let us wait and see what happens."

Something happened very quickly. While we were talking a young man entered the store and came up to me.

"I understand that you are a minister," he said.

"Yes," I replied. "What can I do for you?"

"You can marry me to the best woman in Alaska."

"Is she here?" I asked, with a triumphant smile at Fickus.

"Oh, yes; she came on the last boat from Seattle."

"When do you wish the ceremony to take place?" I inquired.

"Right now," he replied. "You can't tie the knot too quickly to suit me."

I followed the eager young man, married him to a nice-looking girl who was waiting in a near-by cabin, received a wedding-fee of twenty dollars, and returned to my newly-found friend with the assurance that my wants were supplied until my outfit would come ashore.

This was my introduction to the second great gold camp of the Northwest—the raw, crazy, confused stampede of Nome.

II

THE ANVIL

THE first two great gold camps of the Northwest were very different, although largely composed of the same material. In physical features they were most unlike. The Klondike was in the great, beautiful, mountainous, forested Interior; Nome was on the bleak, treeless, low, exposed coast of Bering Sea. To reach the Klondike you steamed from Seattle through twelve hundred miles of the wonderful "Inside Passage," broke through the chain of snowy mountains by the Chilcoot Pass, and, in your rough rowboat, shot down the six hundred miles of the untamed and untameable Yukon. Or else you sailed twenty-three hundred miles over the heaving Pacific and the choppy Bering Sea to St. Michael, and then steamed laboriously against the stiff current of the same Father Yukon eighteen hundred miles *up* to Dawson. To reach Nome you simply steamed the twenty-three hundred miles of Pacific Ocean and Bering Sea; or, if you were up the Yukon, came down it to St. Michael and across Norton Sound a hundred and fifty miles to Nome.

Though on the same parallel of north latitude, the climates of the two camps are very unlike. In the Klondike you have the light, dry, *hot* air of summer; the light, dry, *cold* air of winter. There are long periods when the sky is cloudless. In the summer of unbroken day the land drowses, bathed in warm sunshine and humming with insect life, no breath of air shaking the aspens; in the winter of almost unbroken but luminous night, the Spirit of the North broods like James Whitcomb Riley's Lugubrious Whing-whang,

> "Crouching low by the winding creeks,
> And holding his breath for weeks and weeks."

There are no wind-storms in the Klondike, and a blanket of fine, dry snow covers the land in unvarying depth of only a foot or two.

On Seward Peninsula, the Spirit of Winter breathes hard, and hurls his snow-laden blasts with fearful velocity over the icy wastes. The snow falls to great depth, and never lies still in one place. It drifts, and will cover your house completely under in one night, and pack so hard that the Eskimo can drive his reindeer team over your roof in the morning. The air becomes so full of the flying particles that you cannot see the lead-dog of your team. Men have lost their way in the streets of Nome and wandered out on the tundra to their death. There is considerable sunshine in the summer, and some comparatively still days, but there is much rain, and mossy swamps are everywhere.

The men at Nome in the fall of '99 included many who had been at Dawson in '97, but conditions were very different. The Klondike Stampede was composed of tenderfeet, not one in twenty of whom had ever mined for anything before—men of the city and village and workshop and farm, new to wilderness life, unused to roughing it. Those who reached Nome in '99 were mostly victims of hard luck. Many were Klondikers who had spent two winters rushing wildly from creek to creek on fake reports, possessing themselves of a multitude of worthless claims, eating up the outfits they had brought in with them, and then working for wages in mines of the lucky ones to buy a passage to the new diggings. Many had come down the Yukon in their own rowboats.

But the Klondike Stampede was the cause of other smaller but more fruitless stampedes. These were started by steamboat companies, or by trading companies, and often by "wildcat" mining companies, and were generally cruel hoaxes. Scores of small steamboats, hastily built for the purpose, went up the Yukon to the Koyakuk and other tributaries in the summer of '98. Other scores of power-schooners and small sailing vessels sailed through Bering Strait into the Arctic Ocean and through Kotzebue Sound to the Kobuk and Sewalik Rivers. Almost without exception these eager gold- seekers of '98 found only disappointment, endured the savage winter as best they could, and, out of money and food, were making their way back to the States, when news of the marvelous "beach diggings" at Nome met them and they flocked thither in hopes of at least making back their "grub-stake."

As these vessels approached the new camp, the most prominent landmark which met their eyes was a lone rock in the shape of an anvil, which crowned the summit of the highest of the hills near the coast. At the base of this hill rich gold diggings were found in a creek. The town which sprung up was first called Anvil City; but the Government postal authorities, looking at the map, found Cape Nome in the vicinity, and the post-office was named after the Cape.

Anvil Rock. Overlooking Nome

For the name "Nome" two explanations are given. It is said that theAmerican and Canadian surveyors who were laying out the projected Western Union Telegraph Line across the American and Asiatic Continents, failed to find a name for this cape and wrote it down "No name," which was afterwards shortened to Nome. The more probable explanation is that the surveyors asked an Eskimo the name of the cape. Now the Eskimo negative is "No-me," and the man not understanding, or not knowing its name said "No-me." This was written down and put on the map as the name.

But I like Anvil, and spoke and voted for that name at the first town meeting, held soon after I landed at the new camp. For the camp has been a place of hard knocks from the first. Rugged men have come there to meet severe conditions and have been hammered and broken by the blows of adversity. Others have been shaped and moulded by fiery trial and "the bludgeonings of chance." When I see that stone anvil I think of Tennyson's inspired lines:

"For life is not an idle ore,
But iron, dug from central gloom,
  And heated hot with burning fears,
  And dipt in baths of hissing tears,
And battered with the shocks of doom,
To shape and use."

I was battered as hard as any one on this anvil of the Northwest; but to-day I feel nothing but gratitude for the severe experience.

I had to wait until Saturday before the little steamer on which I came from St. Michael returned from the shelter of Sledge Island and put my goods ashore. In the meantime I had obtained permission to spread my blankets on the floor of the Alaska Exploration Company's store. During that first week we had constant storms. Five or six vessels were driven ashore and broken up by the violence of the waves.

But I was getting my congregation together, and so was happy. A goodly proportion of Christian men and women are always found in these gold camps, and they are very willing workers. Before Sunday came I had found an old acquaintance, Minor Bruce, whom I had known fifteen years before when he was a trader in Southeastern Alaska. He offered me the use of the loft over his fur store. Mr. Fickus, the man from San Francisco, to whom I have made reference in a former chapter, fixed up some seats. I got my organ carried up the ladder and found singers. "Judge" McNulty, a lawyer friend who was handy with crayons, made fancy posters out of some pasteboard boxes I had got from the store.

The floor of Bruce's store was cluttered with Eskimo mucklucks, bales of hair-seal skins, and other unsavory articles; and an old Eskimo woman, who had her lower lip and chin tattooed downwards in streaks after the fashion of these people, sat among the skins, chewing walrus hides and shaping them into soles for mucklucks, while the congregation was gathering. One usher received the people at the store door, steered them carefully between the bales and skins, and headed them to another who helped them up the steep stairway, while a third seated them. We had a good congregation and a rousing meeting. Our choir was one of the best I ever heard. Our organist and leader was Dr. Humphrey, a dentist, who had been director of a large chorus and choir; Mr. Beebe, our chief baritone, had sung in the choir of St. Paul's Episcopal Church of Oakland, Cal.; and there were other professionals. I give these details as a typical beginning in a frontier camp. There is always fine talent of all sorts in a new gold town.

Let me give right here two or three instances of the bread of kindness "cast upon the waters" and "found after many days." Nowhere is this Bible saying oftener realized than in the friendly wilderness.

One of the first men I met at Nome was an old Colorado miner, whom I had known at Dawson. I had done him some kindness at the Klondike camp during the illness and after the death of his nephew. When he found me at Nome he greeted me warmly. "You're just the man I've been looking for. I know you don't do any mining, but I'm going to do some for you. I expect to go ‘outside’ in a few days. You come out on the tundra with me to-morrow, and I’ll stake some ground for you; then I’ll take your papers out with me and try to sell the claims.”

I went with him and he marked off three claims for me, which he had already selected. The next spring, when my long illness had plunged me deeply into debt and I was wondering how I could pay my obligations, my old friend returned with a thousand dollars, from the sale of one of my claims. I paid my doctor’s bills and the other debts, and rejoiced. It was as money thrown down to me from heaven, in my time of dire need.

At Dawson, in the summer of ‘98, I helped an old G. A. R. man from Missouri. He had been sick with the scurvy and was drowned out by the spring freshets and driven to the roof of his cabin, where I found him helpless and half-devoured by mosquitoes. I raised money for his need and sent him out home by one of the first steamboats down the Yukon. Before he left he pressed upon me the only gift he could offer—a fine Parker shotgun. I took this gun with me when I went to stake my claims and bagged a lot of ptarmigan; and a number of times afterwards I shot others of these delicious wild chickens with it. And when I was taken ill and my money all spent, I was able to sell the gun for a goodly sum.

One more link in this chain of kindness: When my goods came ashore and I was able to set up my tent, I found two men, one a Norwegian, the other a Michigander, both of whom had just arrived, without a shelter. I took them into my tent. They helped me to move my goods, made me a cot and fixed up tables, box-chairs and shelves for me. The Norwegian was a very fine cook and baked my “shickens” for me most deliciously. I kept the men in my tent until they could build a cabin. When I became ill they would come to see me, bringing ptarmigan broth and other delicacies; and when I was convalescing and ravenous the Norwegian came again and again to my cabin, bringing “shickens for Mr. Zhung,” and roasted them for me, serving them with his famous nut-butter gravy. In the language of the Northwest, “I didn’t do a thing to those chickens.” Of all places in the world, I think Alaska is most fruitful in return for little acts of kindness.

Men such as I have just described were pure metal, and the heavy blows they received on the anvil only made their characters more beautiful and efficient.

It was in the metal of the men themselves—what this hard life would do for them. Some it made—some it ruined. Among the “Lucky Swedes,” who leaped in a few months from poverty to wealth by the discovery of gold in Anvil Creek, three form a typical illustration.

One was a missionary to the Eskimos, on a small salary. At first his gold gave him much perplexity and trouble while he was being shaped to fit new conditions; but he rose finely to the occasion, gave a large part of his wealth to his church board for building missions and schools among the natives, and pursued his Christian way, honored and beloved, to broader paths of greater usefulness.

A second Swede was also a missionary, teaching the little Eskimos on a salary of six hundred dollars a year. His gold completely turned his head. He fell an easy prey to designing men and women. He became dissipated and broken in body and character. He tried to keep for his own use the gold taken from the claim he had staked in the name of his Mission. His Board sued him for their rights. Long litigation, in which he figured as dishonest, selfish and grasping, followed, his church getting only a small part of its dues. The last I heard of him he was a mere wreck of a man, disgraced, despised and shunned by his former friends. The anvil battering, the trial by fire, the hard blows, proved him base metal.

The third man was a Swedish sailor and longshoreman, ignorant and low, living a hand-to-mouth, sordid life, with no prospects of honor or wealth. His gold at first plunged him into a wild orgy of gambling and dissipation. He took the typhoid fever and was taken "outside." Everybody prophesied that he would simply "go the pace" to complete destruction.

But there was true steel in his composition. His moral fiber stiffened. He began to think and study. He broke away from his drunken associates. He sought the companionship of the cultured. A good woman married and educated him. He has become one of Alaska's wealthiest and most influential citizens, and his charities abound. The stern anvil shaped him to world- usefulness. It is all in the *man*!

Here at Nome I first made the acquaintance of that strange race in which I afterwards became so much interested—the Eskimo. At first they were a source of considerable annoyance. I always felt like laughing aloud when the queer, fat, dish-faced, pudgy folk came in sight. As we had to depend upon driftwood for our fuel, they would come several times a day, bringing huge basketfuls of the soggy sticks for sale at fifty cents a basket.

They soon learned that I was a missionary, and then they would come rolling along, forty or fifty of them at a time, and "bunch up" in front of my tent. If I were cooking dinner they were sure to gather in full force, and would lift up the flap of my tent, grinning at me and eyeing every mouthful I ate. I did not know enough of their language even to tell them to go away. Their rank native odors were overpowering in the hot tent. You could detect the presence of one of those fellows half a mile away if the wind were blowing from him to you. The combined smells of a company of natives, not one of whom had ever taken a bath in his or her life, and who lived upon ancient fish and "ripe" seal blubber—well, I'll stop right here!

One evening at a social in our warehouse-church we played the "limerick" game, which was then a popular craze. We would take a word and each one would write a verse on it. One of the words was Esquimaux. A number of the "limericks" were published in the *Nome Nugget*. With a man's usual egotism I can only remember my own, which I saw at intervals for several years in Eastern periodicals:

"Oh, look at this queer Esquimaux!
His nose is too pudgy to blaux.
    His odors are awful;
    To tell them unlawful.
The thought of them fills me with waux."

One day I was getting dinner in my tent and the usual company of natives watching the performance, when there came along a couple of men who had just landed and who, evidently, had never seen an Eskimo before. I overheard their conversation.

"Say, Jim," said one, "just look there. Did you ever see the like?" (A pause.) "Say, do you think them things has souls?"

"We-e-ll," drawled Jim, "I reckon they must have. They're human bein's. But I'll tell you this: If they do, they've all got to go to heaven, sure; for the devil'd never have them around."

Now let me tell you a sequel: Two years afterwards I was a Commissioner from the newly organized Presbytery of Yukon to the General Assembly, which met at Philadelphia. My fellow Commissioner from the Presbytery—the elder who sat by my side—was Peter Koonooya, an Eskimo elder from Ukeavik Church, Point Barrow. Ten years earlier, Dr. Sheldon Jackson, then Superintendent of Education for Alaska, had visited that northernmost point of the Continent and had started a school and mission. Peter Koonooya was one of the fruits. He was a native of extraordinary intelligence, a man of property, owning a fleet of whaling *oomiaks*. He could read, write and talk English, was a constant student of the Bible, and was considered by the Presbytery of sufficient intelligence and piety to represent us in the supreme Council of the Church.

I am quite certain that Peter always voted exactly right on all questions which were up before that Assembly; because he watched me very closely and voted as I did.

I was able, then, and in after years, to do these gentle, good-natured natives some good, and other Christian teachers have done much more for them. So it comes about that the condition of the Alaska Eskimo, under the influence of the various Christian missions and schools among them, as compared with that of their brothers and sisters of the same race across Bering Strait in Asia, for whom nothing in a Christian way has been done, is as day to night. They are pliable metal, and the Anvil of the Northwest is shaping them into vessels and implements of usefulness and honor.

The Odoriferous but Interesting Eskimo

Two of Dr. Young's Parishioners

III

BUNCH-GRASS BILL

ALTHOUGH I had often met him on the streets of Dawson in '98, I had not come into hand-shaking contact with Bunch-grass Bill until my first week at Nome. Of all the social orders whose members gathered together in clubs for humane work during the epidemic of typhoid fever, the first to organize, besides being the strongest and most active, was the Odd Fellows' Club. It was already organized when I arrived and, as I belonged to the order, I was present at the second meeting. The young lawyer who was president of the Club, taking me around the little circle of earnest men, brought me to a black- haired, black-eyed, sturdily-built and singularly handsome young Irishman by the name of Billy Murtagh.

"Billy owns and runs the 'Beach Saloon,' and goes by the name of Bunch-grass Bill," introduced our president. "I don't know how he got into the Odd Fellows, under rules which bar saloon-keepers and bad men. But he's in, and we'll not turn him out of the Club, at least so long as this distress continues."

Bill made no reply to this rather uncomplimentary introduction, but shook hands with Irish heartiness and looked at me with level gaze. "I've seen you in my saloon at Dawson," he said.

The others laughed, and the president chided, "You oughtn't to give a preacher away like that, Bill."

Taking a closer look at the young man, a scene at Dawson a year earlier flashed upon me. I was collecting money to pay the passage on the steamboat bound down the Yukon of some poor fellows who were broken and sick, and who must go "outside" or die. I made the round of the saloons and gambling halls, and going into one of these places was curtly refused by one of the partners. The other, who was this young man, came up and quietly said to the cashier, "Weigh him out two ounces ($32.00)."

"Oh, I remember you now, and your two ounces," I said to Bill; and to the others, "I can vouch for his knowing the Second Degree of the order, at least."

I was made chairman of the Relief Committee of the Club, and found work a-plenty cut out for me. Although the members of the Club did not look with indifference upon any case of distress, yet its prime object was to look up and help the sick Odd Fellows. I prepared a bulletin and tacked it up in the stores and saloons, directing that any cases of distress among the members of the order should be reported to the Committee. As the typhoid epidemic increased in virulence, the Club found its hands full.

A day or two after this first meeting, I was passing Bill's saloon when he called me in.

"I've just heard of a sick man," he reported, "and I think he's an Odd Fellow." Then, after a pause, he added, "But if he isn't that doesn't make a —— bit of difference."

He led the way along the beach for half a mile or more, to an isolated tent, where we found the typhoid case. Billy stayed until he made sure that the man was well cared for in the charge of friends and a good physician. Then he took me aside and slipped a twenty-dollar gold piece into my hand. "Use that for him," he directed.

The next day I had to raise a hundred and fifty dollars to send an old miner who was poor and crippled "outside." I marched at once to the "Beach Saloon." "Billy," I said, "this old-timer has blown in all his dust for booze; and it's up to you who have got it from him to take care of him now."

"That's right," he promptly answered. "There's ten saloons; what would be my share?"

"An ounce," I replied, passing him the paper.

He weighed out the gold dust. "Wait a while before going on. I'll pass the word down the line," he said.

Half an hour afterwards I stopped again at his door. "They're all ready," reported Bill. "If any of them guys don't come across, just tell me."

They all "came across," and thereafter, until I left Nome, all the saloon-keepers met every demand I made upon them without question. When a man had been impoverished or made sick through drink I went to the saloons, *only*, for his relief. In other cases I made a general canvass. When collecting money for church purposes I went to everybody, *except* the saloon-keepers and their following.

The day before my second meeting with the Odd Fellows' Club—a rainy, blustering day—I came to Bunch-grass Bill with a greater demand.

"It is you I want this time, Billy, not just your money," I said. "There is a sick Odd Fellow in a tent almost a mile from here. He is alone and lying in a puddle of water. Get your gum-boots and find three or four other stout men and come with me."

Bill agreed at once, found a man to tend his bar, secured a squad of strong and willing men, a stretcher from the army post and a good physician and went with me on the errand of mercy. He worked all day in the mud and rain. He carried the sick man to the warehouse which we had turned into a temporary hospital, visited all the stores in an attempt to find mattresses, and, failing in that, bought eight large reindeer skins and piled them on the floor for a bed, bought underwear, dry blankets and other comforts for the sick man, and laid in a supply of delicacies for the use of the hospital. In all, he spent over fifty dollars and a whole day of strenuous work upon the case.

When I asked him at dusk if he were not tired he laughed: "Never had a better time in all my life."

That night was the regular weekly meeting of the Club. I made my report, which was quite long, and mentioned many distressing cases, showing an alarming increase of the typhoid. Then I asked for a rotary relief committee of three to be chosen at every other meeting, and a permanent relief committee of two.

"I've found the biggest-hearted man in all Alaska," I said. "His business and mine are not quite the same. In fact I have been all my life fighting saloons and saloon-keepers, and I expect to keep on fighting them until I die. But this man's heart of love for his fellow-men fights his business harder than I can."

Then I related some of the things Billy had done during the past week, and ended my speech by asking that he be put on the permanent relief committee with me. "We two will find the sick and cut out the work for the rest of you," I promised.

The Club applauded, much to the confusion of Bill, who tried his best to shrink out of sight. One of the boys reported next morning.

"Say, Doctor," he began, "you sure scared Bunch-grass Bill near to death last night. Tickled, too. He asked us all to come in and have one on him. He doesn't know anything else to do when he feels good. 'That's a new one on me,' he said. 'I never had anything to do with a preacher in my life. Didn't like 'em. Kept shy of 'em. But if Father Young sees fit to come into my saloon—and he's in it every day—I'll go with him wherever he wants me to go—even if it's to his church.'"

That touched me, for I could sense something of the sacrifice it would involve. It would be far easier for Bill to start on a three-thousand-mile winter mush on snow-shoes, over unbroken trails, than to step inside of a Protestant meeting-house.

From that time on, Bill was my right hand. As the number of typhoid victims increased, he made his saloon an intelligence office, finding and reporting to me all new cases. The example of the Odd Fellows stimulated the various social orders represented in the camp—the Masons, Knights of Pythias, Elks, Eagles, and others—to a like humane work; and Bill looked up their sick members and reported to their committees. He saw that all the sick had medical attention, and guaranteed the payment of scores of doctor's bills. Each steamboat that left Nome for the "outside" carried a number of convalescents and broken-down and moneyless men, and funds had to be raised for their passage. Bill headed nearly all of these subscription lists, as well as those for fitting up the four temporary hospitals we opened and filled with sick men.

Being for over six weeks the only clergyman in that whole region, I conducted all the funerals. One week I had eleven—all typhoid cases. Bill attended them all, looking after the digging of the graves and making coffins, and often acting as undertaker.

Now, I am not setting up my saloon friend as a saint. Quite the contrary. I suppose he had been guilty of every crime mentioned in the Decalogue. He had never known any home life, but had knocked about from camp to camp of the western frontiers ever since boyhood. His ideas of morality, therefore, were very vague. He was said to have been "run out" of several towns in Montana and Idaho. He had a violent temper and, as the phrase went, was "quick on the trigger." Rumor said that he had the blood of more than one man on his hands; although it was claimed, in every case, that he had not sought the quarrel. He sold whiskey and drank it, gambled and swore habitually without a thought of any of these things being wrong. He was simply an uncultured, ignorant, rough-and-ready, Irish-American backwoodsman.

But to those of us in the raw camp of Nome who witnessed Bill's untiring kindness and self-sacrifice during those weeks of distress, his faults faded into the background behind the light of his many good deeds. St. Peter says, "Charity covers a multitude of sins," and surely Bill's charity "abounded" overwhelmingly, putting out of sight much of the evil in his life.

As for me, I shall always think of him as one of the most loyal, devoted friends I ever had, and the saver of my life. For after seven weeks of most strenuous and wearing work, I was suddenly stricken down with the typhoid myself. The blow came when I was fairly drowned in the multitude of my duties. I was raising the money to send out on the steamboat four or five men who must leave the country or die—poor fellows whose vitality was so low that they could not combat the cold and storms of a Nome winter. I was also preparing another warehouse-hospital. So great was the demand for space for the care of the sick that I had felt compelled to take into my own ten-by- twelve tent three men sick with the disease. So crowded was the tent that I had to sleep under the bed of one of them. Billy Murtagh and others of the Odd Fellows' Club warned me against thus exposing myself to the infection, but there seemed to be no other way. Billy brought me all his remaining Apollinaris water that I might not have to drink the impure seepage of the tundra. Some of the brothers carried me pails of water from the one well which had been recently put down.

While I was in the midst of the canvass for funds, and in the bustle of preparation for the departure of the last steamboats, I had a terrific headache for several days. I was besieged day and night by friends of sick men for places to put the stricken ones where they could be cared for. The life of a number of these men seemed to depend on my keeping on my feet. I had no *time* to be sick. I kept away from Billy and my other friends, for fear they might forcibly interfere.

But one of the Odd Fellows saw me as I was coming out of a store with a subscription paper in my hand. He looked at me for a moment and hurried to the "Beach Saloon."

"Bill," he shouted, "get a doctor, quick, and go to the parson. I saw him just now staggering along with his face as red as fire and his hand to his head. He's got the fever, sure."

Billy came running down the beach with Dr. Davy at his heels and caught me as I was entering my tent. Without ceremony they picked up the sick man who was in my cot and carried him to another tent near by. Then, in spite of my protests, they undressed me and laid me in my blankets. I was half delirious and stubborn. I fought them.

"This is all nonsense, Doctor," I protested. "I have only a headache. There is no time to fool away. These men must go out on this steamboat, and the money is not raised. Let me alone."

Dr. Davy finished his examination and turned to Bunch-grass Bill. "He has a bad case of typhoid," was his verdict, "and ought to have been in bed three or four days ago. Find a house to put him in and a woman to nurse him."

Bill had one of the softest and sweetest voices I ever heard. He came to me and laid his cool hand on my forehead. "Don't you worry about those men, Father," he said gently. "I'll attend to that. Now who do you want to nurse you?"

"Mrs. Perrigo," I replied. "She has just built a new cabin. I helped her with it. Her husband is recovering from the fever."

Soon the good woman was in my tent, eager to serve. I was carried through a driving snow-storm to her cabin. It was a rude affair built of rough boards set upright and battened with narrow, half-inch strips. A single thickness of building-paper poorly supplemented the inch boards. But cold and uncomfortable as it was, it was the only available shelter. I had them bring my tent and make a storm-shed of it in front of the door. There, for more than two months, I was to lie helpless.

My friends told me afterwards of the consternation that my illness caused. I was chairman of all the general relief committees—those of the town council, the citizens, the mission, the Odd Fellows. That the leader should thus be laid aside seemed a greater calamity than was actually the case. For Mr. Wirt of the Congregational Church arrived with lumber to erect a hospital, and Raymond Robins, a young man of great earnestness and talent, who has since arisen to national prominence, came with him to help in Christian work.

The night after I was taken to the Perrigo cabin, there was a meeting of the Odd Fellows' Club. Billy Murtagh was present and made his first public speech. As my illness and the general situation was discussed he rose to his feet, the tears streaming down his face. He seemed unconscious of them—or, at least, unashamed.

"Fellers," he faltered, "I'm hard hit. This gets me where I live. Now I'll tell you this: you fellers can look after the other sick folks, and call on me when you need any money. But I want you to leave Father Young to me. I've adopted him. He's my father. All I've got is his. If there's anything in this camp he needs, he's goin' to have it."

Ah, that long, desperate fight for life! The stunning pain in my head, the high fever, the delirium, the nervous terror, the deadly weakness, the emaciation, the chills and nausea! I was badly handicapped in my fight. The two months of wearing work and strain which preceded my illness had exhausted me, body and mind—there was no vital reserve to draw upon.

I was in a little, cold shanty, twelve feet square, crowded and unhealthy. Two people besides myself must live in that tiny room—sleep there, cook there. The savage arctic winter raged against us, howling his vengeance upon our impudence in thus braving him, unprepared. He made every nail-head inside the house a knob of frost. When my blankets, damp with the steam of cooking, touched the wall, he clamped them so tight one must tear the fabric in pulling it free. He made my clothing, stowed under the cot, a solid lump of ice. He asphyxiated us with foul gases when the door was closed, and filled the room instantly with fine snow from the condensation of the moisture when it was opened. He charged constantly upon the thin shell of the house with his high October and November winds, shaking it wildly and threatening to bowl it over. He drove, in horizontal sheets, the fine, flour-like snow, shooting it through batten-crevice, door-crack and keyhole; and, finding myriad small apertures in the shake roof, sifted it down upon my face. He piled it in fantastic whirls around the house, selecting the side on which our one small window was, to bank it highest, so that he might shut out our light. He sent the red spirit in the thermometer tube down, down, down—ten below zero, twenty, thirty when it stormed, and forty, fifty, sixty below when it was still, and the black death-mist brooded over the icy wastes and men breathed ice-splinters instead of air.

The fuel supply for the Nome camp was very poor and scanty. Men were digging old, sodden logs of driftwood out of the snow, and hauling this sorry fire-wood twenty miles by hand. Coal was scarce and sold by the ton for $150.00, or by the bucket for ten cents a pound.

Having had experience with typhoid epidemics and other sicknesses in the Klondike Stampede, I had laid in a good supply of nice foods for the sick, such as malted milk, the best brands of condensed milk, tapioca, farina, and other delicacies; but all of these had been given away before my own illness, and there was a scarcity of such articles in the stores.

But my friends, women and men,—indeed, everybody in the camp seemed interested in me and anxious to do something for me—arose to meet all these emergencies and "ministered to mine infirmities." The Odd Fellows supplemented the efforts of the convalescent, but still shaky Perrigo, and cut the wind-packed snow into bricks and built it around the house, until it looked like a veritable Eskimo igloo. It was much warmer after this was done.

The doctors at Nome all prescribed a diet of milk and whiskey for their fever patients. Upon the news of my illness circulating in the camp a dozen bottles of different brands were at once sent to me. Billy came, examined, smelled at, and tasted these liquors, with the air of an expert. Then he bundled all the bottles into a gunny sack and carried them away, saying, "He's not going to have any of this dope. I've got some of the pure stuff, made in Ireland." And he brought me an ample supply for all my needs, and a gallon of pure alcohol for sponge-baths.

The Odd Fellows organized wood-cutting "bees" for my benefit, and daily carried water from the well for Mrs. Perrigo's use. The women collected food and milk from their own stores and those of others, and brought them to me. The fellowship of the wilderness, the finest in the world, had its full exercise for my benefit there at Nome. I doubt if there was a person in all that great camp who would not have given me cheerfully his last can of milk.

As the fever progressed and my condition grew more serious, the daily visitors were restricted to two—Mrs. Strong and Bunch-grass Bill. The lady looked after matters of business, my letters, and information about other sick people. Billy, with his soft, low voice and gentle manner, hovered over me, sitting for hours at my bedside, lifting me in his two big hands with infinite care and deftness. Never did son care for father with more tender solicitude and fuller devotion than did this Irish Catholic saloon-keeper, this "bad man" of the western frontier, for me—a Protestant preacher.

There were many malamute dogs at Nome, great, beautiful, wolf-like beasts, and the "malamute chorus" was much in evidence in the late hours of the night. One, in particular, which was tied up not far from Perrigo's cabin, tuned up regularly every morning at three o'clock with his high-pitched tremolo, waking every dog within a mile, until all were howling, and keeping it up till daylight. There was no sleep possible for me while this concert was in progress, and I used to lie awake for hours, waiting fearfully for the leader to begin, and to cower in my robes with nervous chills coursing down my spine at every renewal of the long-drawn cadence, "Oo-o-o-o-o, oo-o-o-o-o, ow, ow, ow, ow."

My fever would always rise with the commencement of this discordant chorus and increase as long as it continued, and the doctor on his morning visit would find me exhausted and trembling. The words of Clarence would chase each other through my brain:

> "With that, methought, a legion of foul fiends
> Environ'd me, and howled in mine ears
> Such hideous cries, that, with the very noise
> I trembling wak'd, and, for a season after
> Could not believe but what I was in hell."

Mrs. Perrigo told Billy of the nuisance. He stayed up that night until the leading canine musician shrieked his solo to the moon. He followed up the sound until he found the dog, roused the grumbling owner, paid the high price asked for the animal, led him down the beach half a mile, and shot him.

An errand of an opposite character also fell to Billy's lot. The barracks which housed a squadron of United States soldiers was less than a block from the cabin in which I lay. Every night at eleven o'clock a bugle of remarkable sweetness and expression would blow "Taps." I would listen for the soothing melody, and when it would sound I would turn over in my robe and obey its command, "Go-o-o to sle-e-ep."

Lieutenant Craig, the commander of the post, ordered the discontinuance of "Taps," thinking it would disturb me and the other sick people. That night I waited, as usual, for the "good-night" bugle, and when it did not sound I grew anxious and distraught. I thought my watch was wrong or the bugler must be sick. I grew excited, restless and feverish, and passed a sleepless night, missing my accustomed lullaby. We told Billy; he went to see the Lieutenant, and the next night the lovely, soothing phrase sounded forth on the still night air, and I slept.

TAPS.
Listen

Another cause of nervousness and anxiety arose, requiring the efforts of both Mrs. Strong and Billy Murtagh to solve the difficulty. I was paying my nurse, Mrs. Perrigo, five dollars a day, which was almost all she and her husband had to live on. They had been eating for a year and a half a food outfit designed for only a single season, and there was but little of it left. Mr. Perrigo, who was a Yankee tintype-picture peddler and knew no other trade, had tried his best to be a gold-miner; but, in common with the rest of the forlorn "Kobuckers," had made nothing at all. His wife, who had been a bookkeeper in Boston, valiantly took up the trades of waitress, washerwoman and cook in the Arctic wilderness, but there was but little money in that disappointed crowd. Almost immediately after landing on the "golden sands" of Nome in August Mr. Perrigo was stricken with the fever. With the fearful prices that prevailed, my five dollars a day was little enough to feed them and meet the monthly payments on their house.

I had accumulated $125.00—mostly wedding fees—when I was taken sick. It melted away like a spoonful of sugar in a cup of hot coffee. Every Monday I must have thirty-five dollars for my faithful nurse. I placed in Mrs. Strong's hands for sale my Parker shotgun, my typewriter, my gold-scales, my extra overcoat, all gifts from friends. She got good prices for them, and for the few articles I could spare from my food supply—but still the phantom weekly payment menaced me. When I closed my eyes the figures—$35.00—big and lurid—stared at me, and in my delirious dreams became red goblins, mocking me.

A splendid woman, member of the church which assumed my salary, had given me two beautiful wolf robes. I was lying in the heavier one. I delivered the other to Mrs. Strong. "Sell it for me," I requested. "You ought to get fifty or sixty dollars for it."

A week passed—then another. Mrs. Strong reported she "was holding the robe for a higher price." The crisis I had dreaded had arrived. My money was gone. I had none to meet next Monday's payment.

"Sell the robe for what it will bring," I directed Mrs. Strong. "I must have the money."

"I'll sell it on Saturday," she promised.

Monday morning Mrs. Strong marched in with a large canvas money-bag in her hand. With Mrs. Perrigo's assistance she counted out the money, which was mostly in silver coins. Then she wrote in large figures, "$158.50," and pinned the paper on the wall by my head.

"Where on earth did you get that money?" I cried.

"Why, for the robe, of course."

"You never got all that for it."

"Yes, I did," she affirmed.

Then the truth dawned upon me. "Mrs. Strong!" I exclaimed, "you raffled the robe!"

"Yes," she laughed. "What are you going to do about it?"

Then she explained. Finding it impossible to get a fair price for the fur blanket she and Bunch-grass Bill had laid their heads together. They knew that I would not consent to a raffle, so they kept the matter quiet. Bill displayed the robe in front of his saloon. Shares were offered at fifty cents each. My lady friends of the mission sold tickets. Bill bought fifty and others of my friends did almost as well. Their purpose if they won the robe was to give it back to me.

What could I do? To rebuke their kindly deception would be ungracious indeed. With brimming eyes I thanked my friends, and Mrs. Perrigo got her money.

But the greatest of Bunch-grass Bill's many acts of kindness towards me remains to be told. As Dr. Davy had said from the first, mine was "a bad case." I had seven and a half weeks of high fever before it broke, whereas the usual limit of fever was three weeks. I reached the extreme of emaciation and weakness. I could hardly lift my hand. When they bundled me in a blanket like a baby and hung me on the hook of a big steelyard I weighed sixty pounds! I was long in the Valley of the Shadow of Death and reached its utmost boundary, until the very waters of the dark river lapped my feet.

"Well, Bill," said Dr. Davy with a sigh, as he was returning one morning from his call upon me, and stopped, as was his custom, to report to the "Beach Saloon," "I'm afraid it's about over. I don't think Dr. Young can last much longer. He can retain nothing on his stomach. We've tried all the brands of condensed milk in the camp to no avail. Everything comes up the instant it is swallowed. There are many internal complications, and he may go off any hour in one of those deathly convulsive chills."

"Big Wilbur," who reported the scene to me afterwards, said that Bill's face "went white as chalk, and then flushed red as fire." He jumped at the doctor as though he were going to assault him.

"By God," he cried, "he's not goin' to die. We'll not let him, Doc. See here: When I had the fever at Dawson, what saved me was cow's milk. Now, there's a cow here. You come with me, and we'll go see her."

"That cow," explained Wilbur, "was a wonderful animal. Her owner sold twenty gallons of milk a day from her, and she didn't look as if she gave one. Bill knew the owner was doping the milk with condensed milk and corn- starch and water and other stuff. So he strapped on his two big guns. He's great for bluff, is Bill. Doc. and I went along to see the fun. We found the owner in the stable 'tending to his cow. Bill didn't beat around the bush any.

"'You look here' he said. 'Your cow's givin' too darned much milk. Now this man I want it for is my father, an' he's got enough microbes in him already. Doc. here, analyzed your milk; didn't you, Doc?' (Doc. Davy was game, and nodded.) 'He says you put tundra water and all kinds of dope in it. I'm goin' to keep tab on you, an' if you dope my milk—well, you know *me*! It don't make no difference what you charge—a dollar a bottle or five dollars a bottle —my father's got to have pure milk. Understand?'"

For three months Billy went to the stable every day and superintended the milking. At a cost to him, sometimes, of three dollars for a pint bottle, and never less than a dollar a bottle, the "bad man" brought me every day, with his own hands, a bottle of fresh milk. When Bill and the doctor came in with that first bottle Mrs. Perrigo carefully raised my head and gave me a brimming glass of the rich milk. I drank it all and dropped off to sleep. I needed no more whiskey. The turning point of my illness was that glass of cow's milk. Bill's big bluff saved my life!

To show the rough, yet fine sentiment of the man, let me tell one last word about the lone cow. She went dry before spring, and, as the camp was crazy for fresh meat, the owner butchered her. One of the Odd Fellows told me. Said he, "Bill just went wild when he heard of it, and we had all we could do to keep him from going gunning for the man who killed the cow that saved your life. Why, that man would lay down his life for you, and laugh while he was doin' it."

I would I could tell of Bunch-grass Bill's conversion and entire reformation, but this is a true story, and I never heard that he ever got so far as that. This much, however, I am proud to tell. One day in the spring of 1900, when the army of gold-seekers was beginning to land on the "Golden Beach," I was standing with Bill near his saloon. On a sudden impulse I spoke to him.

"Billy," I said, "I love you, but I don't like your business. It's a bad business. See what it has done to lots of good fellows around here. You are too big for that game. I wish you'd drop it and do something that's clean—that doesn't hurt anybody."

Bill made no reply, and I supposed my words had been fruitless. But in a few weeks one of my friends informed me that Bill had sold out and had gone to gold-mining.

"That's good!" I exclaimed. "Did he give any reason?"

"Yes," the man replied, "Bill said you told him to."

When I was returning to Alaska in 1901, I bought a nice buffalo smoking-set at the Pan-American Exposition and took it to Alaska for Bunch-grass Bill. I did not see him, as he was mining at a distance, but I heard of his pride and pleasure as he displayed the gift and talked affectionately of "Father Young." He left Alaska that summer, and I have heard vaguely of his presence in the Nevada gold-fields. But wherever he is, I pray that God may bless and save the Irish saloon-keeper, who loved me and saved my life.

IV

MY DOGS

MUSHING with dogs in Alaska is the worst and the best mode of traveling in all the world—the most joyful and the most exasperating—according to the angle from which you look at it.

Once I was preaching a series of sermons on the Ten Commandments to the miners at Council, a town on Seward Peninsula eighty-five miles east of Nome. I had come to the Third Commandment; and I bore down pretty hard upon the useless and foolish habit of profane swearing.

When I was going home from the meeting, a group of young men stood on the corner waiting for me.

"Come over here, Doctor," called one of the men. "I have a bet with Jim, and I want you to decide it."

I crossed over to the jolly group. "What is your bet?" I asked.

"Why," he replied, "I've bet Jim five dollars that you have never mushed a dog-team."

"Well, you've lost," I answered. "I have driven dogs many times—and never found it necessary to swear at them, either."

Before I go on with my story, perhaps I would better explain that word "mush," as it is used in the Northwest. The word is never used in Alaska as you use it in the East, to denote porridge, or some sort of cereal. There we say "oatmeal" or "corn-meal," or simply "cereal."

In Alaska the word has but one use. It is a corruption of the French *marchez, marche*, which the Canadian *coureurs du bois*, or travelers of the woods, shout at their dogs when urging them along the trail. From *marche* to "mush" is easy. So now, throughout the great Northwest, Canadian or Alaskan, when a man is traveling he is "on a mush." When he is speaking to his dogs, either to drive them out of the house or to urge them along the trail, he shouts "mush!" If he be a good traveler, he is a "great musher." Of all the pet names they used to give me up there, the one of which I was proudest was "The Mushing Parson."

They tell a story, which has the ear-marks of truth, which illustrates this universal use of the word "mush" in the Northwest.

Two miners, who for years had been in the mining camps of Alaska, at last came "outside" to Seattle. In the morning they went to a restaurant for breakfast and took seats at a table. A rather cross-looking waitress came to take their order. "Mush?" she asked. The miners looked at one another in surprise and alarm. The woman waited a while, and when they did not answer she supposed they were deaf and had not heard her question. "Mush?" she screamed. The two men arose and fled. When they got safely to the sidewalk, one said to the other, "Now, what the Sam Hill did she fire us for?"

There are three principal breeds of native dogs found in Alaska—the Husky, the Malamute and the Siberian Dog—all descendants of wolves, with wolfish traits and the wolf's warm coat and powers of endurance. Of these the Malamute is the largest, descended, as he is, from the great gray wolves of the Arctic regions. The Husky seems to be derived from the red wolf of the McKenzie River Valley; while the Siberian Dog has for ancestor the smaller, shorter-legged, heavier-furred Arctic wolf of the Siberian coast. The smaller and more worthless dogs of the southern Alaska Coast, if descended from wolves, must have the coyote as their progenitor—having his lighter and slimmer body and his sneaking, thievish, cowardly disposition.

Everywhere, however, the dog is largely what his master makes him, and these northern wolf-dogs have greatly improved since they have fallen into the hands of white masters. More intelligent breeding, greater care in feeding and more careful training, have made them what they are—the finest, most enduring and most dependable sleigh-dogs in the world.

The dog is by all odds the most valuable animal of the Northwest to the white miner and settler. He is the miner's horse, bicycle, automobile, locomotive, all in one. Life in those wilds would be almost unendurable without him. The miners appreciate this, and cases of cruelty and mistreatment are very rare. In the days of the early gold stampedes the *cheechackos* or tenderfeet, who knew but little about life in the wilderness, and still less about the dogs of the wilderness, sometimes were guilty of abusing their dogs; but this very seldom occurred, and the old-timers always frowned upon, and sometimes punished, cases of cruelty. I remember once holding, with joy, the coat of one of these old-timers at Dawson in the strenuous winter of 1897-8, while he administered a very beautiful and artistic thrashing to a newcomer who was guilty of beating his dogs with a heavy chain and knocking out the eye of one of them.

But I cannot better give you an idea of what dog-mushing in the Northwest is than by sketching a trip I took to a meeting of the Presbytery of Yukon in March, 1912. I was at Iditarod, a new gold-mining town in the western interior of Alaska. The meeting was to be held at Cordova on the southern coast, seven hundred and twenty miles distant. To reach Cordova I must cross four mountain ranges—the Western, the Alaska, the Chugach and the Kenai Ranges; and traverse four great river valleys—the Yukon, the Kuskoquim, the Susitna and the Matanuska. There was first a very rough stretch of rudely marked trail five hundred and twenty miles to Seward. There I would take a steamboat two hundred miles to Cordova. Let us betake ourselves together to this big miner's camp, and talk the matter over in the free, familiar way of the Northwest:

A young fellow of Scotch descent hailing from the north of Ireland, William Breeze, known far and wide as an experienced "dog musher," is to be my companion on this trip. He is bound for Susitna, three hundred miles from Iditarod, on a prospecting trip, and will take care of my dogs, boil their feed at night and do the heaviest part of the work.

Dr. Young and his Dog Team

Iditarod, February, 1912

And now let me introduce you to my team. It is one of the finest teams in all the North. There are five pups of the same litter, now six or seven years old. They are a cross between the McKenzie River husky and the shepherd dog, and have the long hair and hardy endurance of the former and the sagacity, intelligence and affection of the latter. Being brothers, they know each other and are taught to work together, although this fact does not hinder them from engaging in a general free-for-all fight now and again. However, if attacked by strange dogs the whole five work together beautifully, centering their forces with Napoleonic strategy and beating the enemy in detail.

The leader is black, white and tan, marked like a shepherd dog. He has been named "Nigger," but I have changed his name simply to "Leader." It sounds enough like the original to please him and keep him going. He is a splendid leader. He has a swift, swinging pace, and can keep the trail when it is covered a foot deep by fresh snow and there is no external sign of it. He has that intelligence which leads him to avoid dangers, and he will stop and look back at you if there is a hole in the ice or a dangerous slide, awaiting your orders and co-operation before he essays the difficult problem. His knowledge of "Gee" and "Haw" is perfect, the tone in which you pronounce these words and the force with which you utter them telling him just how far to the right, or to the left, he is to swing. "*Gee!*" spoken in a short, explosive, loud tone will turn him square to the right, while "Ge-e-e, ge-e-e-e," in soft lengthened syllables, will make him veer slowly and gradually. His sense of responsibility is very great, and his censorship of the conduct of his fellow teamsters very severe. He will not tolerate any shirking on their part and takes keen delight in their correction when they deserve it. But he will fly at your throat if you touch *him* with the whip.

The "swing dogs" just behind him are "Moose" and "Ring," colored like Irish setters. They have exactly the same gait, are the same size, and almost the same coloring, "Ring" a little lighter than "Moose" and with a white collar around his neck which suggested his name. "Moose" is a little gentleman, the loveliest dog I have ever known. His traces are always taut, and when you utter his name he will jump right up into the air, straining on his collar. He knows the words of command as well as the leader, and has never, perhaps, been touched with the whip. I think chastisement would break his heart, for he would know it was unmerited. He is my pet, the one dog of the team that I allow in my cabin, and my companion in my short journeys through the camp. He is remarkably clean and dainty in his habits, his coat shining like polished bronze. He would guard my person or my coat with his life, the most faithful, intelligent and affectionate dog I have ever had. I love that dog.

"Ring" is also willing, but has not the intelligence or the good nature of "Moose." He is a scrapper and apt to embroil the rest of the team in a general fight. But he will work all day at his highest tension.

"Teddy" and "Sheep," the "wheel dogs," are not so valuable as the other three. "Teddy" has the longest hair and the lightest weight of any, and the least strength; but he is a willing little fellow and a very keen hunter. Make a noise like a squirrel or a bird, and he will prick up his ears and dash down the path after the game, and when a real rabbit or ptarmigan crosses his path he will tear madly along until the game is passed. You can fool him every minute of the day, and Breeze has a way of imitating the little birds that keeps "Teddy" working his hardest.

"Sheep" is a malingerer. He is a clown, and so comical that you cannot help laughing at him, even when you know he deserves a good thrashing. He is fat, heavy and awkward. In color he is a light, tawny yellow, with long hair like "Teddy," but labors under the serious disability of having a different gait from the others. They are pacers; he is a trotter. When they are swinging rhythmically along at a five-mile gait, "Sheep" has to lope, his trot not being equal to the occasion. He has a way of playing off sick or fagged; but if game appears, he forgets all about his pretenses, his lameness is all gone in a second and he is the keenest of the team. Also, when nearing the camp he forgets his weariness and pulls harder than any of the team. It is necessary to let him see the whip constantly, and occasionally to feel it, and he is the only one of the team that necessitates its use at all.

About once a day, on the trail, a funny scene has to be enacted. We may be laboring up a long hill, or wallowing through deep snow, the difficult ascent requiring every man and dog to do his best. "Sheep" will get tired, and, with a backward look at me to see if I am noticing, will let his traces slacken. I give him a touch of the whip, and, although he can hardly feel the lash through his thick coat, he yelps and pulls manfully for a short distance; but presently his trace chain sags again. Soon "Leader" notices the heavier pulling and, knowing where the blame lies, turns his head, shows his teeth and growls at "Sheep," who jumps into his collar and pulls like a good fellow. Soon he forgets and lets up again, getting a fiercer growl from "Leader." A third time he is a slacker. Then "Leader" stops and begins to swing around carefully so as not to tangle the harness. "Moose" and "Ring" and "Teddy" all stand still and look at "Sheep." That unfortunate trotter lies down on his back with his feet in the air and begins to howl in anguish. I sit down on the sled and wait— I know what is coming. "Leader" reaches "Sheep" and for about a minute there is a bedlam of savage growls from "Leader" and piercing shrieks from "Sheep." I notice that "Leader" does not take the culprit by the throat, but only pinches the loose hide on his breast and side. That cannot injure him, so I am not uneasy. The punishment over, "Leader" resumes his place. "Sheep" gets up and shakes himself with an air of relief. I take the handle-bars and call "Mush." For the rest of the day "Sheep" pulls for all he is worth; but the next day he forgets and has to be trounced again.

I am conscious that this story may have a "fishy" flavor for some of my readers, but I can assure them it is true.

But mine are all fine little dogs, not as large as the malamute, but with more courage, spirit and intelligence. The long hair protects them from the cold and they will cuddle down in the snow contentedly, curled up like little shrimps, and let it cover them.

We must take along enough feed for the dogs, to last them from salmon stream to salmon stream. The staple of their feed is dried salmon; it goes a long way for its weight. We start with a hundred pounds of it, and fifty pounds of rice and tallow. This, boiled into a savory mess and served once a day (when they stop for the night), keeps the dogs fat and hearty. We shall replenish the supply at intervals, for five dogs will eat an immense amount of food, and must have all that they can eat at their daily meal.

The sled is a basket-sleigh with handle-bars and brake at the back and a "gee-pole" in front, with an extra rope when we have to "neck it" to help the dogs. My wolf-robe is spread on the floor of the sleigh for my accommodation in the brief intervals of riding. For dog mushing in Alaska does not mean luxuriously riding in your sleigh wrapped up in your fur robe while the dogs haul you along the trail. When Dr. Egbert Koonce sledded twelve hundred miles from Rampart to Valdez in 1902 on his way to the General Assembly, I told the Assembly of the feat. A good friend from Philadelphia said: "It must after all be a really luxurious way of traveling, wrapped up in your furs and reclining in a comfortable sleigh behind your dogs." I turned to Koonce and asked him how much of that twelve hundred miles he rode. "About two miles," he replied.

I shall ride more than this on my way to Seward, but there will not be many places where I can ride half a mile at a stretch without getting out and running behind the dogs. The beauty of "dog mushing" is that you are compelled to work as hard as the dogs. You are not on a well-beaten boulevard; you are wending your way around trees and stumps, over hummocks, up and down hills, along the sides of the mountains, and must keep your hands on the handle-bars, lifting the sled on the trail when it runs off and often breaking the trail ahead with your snow-shoes. When the dogs are on fairly good roads they swing along uninterruptedly and you run your best behind. If there are two of you, one holds the handle-bars and the other sprints along, either in front or behind the sleigh. You will get pretty tired the first two or three days, but after your muscles become hardened and you get your second wind, you can run at your keenest gait two or three miles at a time.

But let us get started. All preparations are made, the supply of dog-feed loaded, our robes and blankets put aboard, heavy canvas corded around the load and our snow-shoes strapped on top. We shall not need a gun, for there will be plenty of game to be had at the roadhouses, and we shall not have time to bother with hunting. We have a long journey to make and everything must bend to getting over the ground. That "ribbon of the trail" must be unwound for five hundred and twenty miles. A company of warm and sympathetic friends foregather to bid us "good-bye," and off we go.

The trail is well beaten from Iditarod to Flat City, seven and a half miles, and I get aboard, with Breeze at the handle-bars. My huskies leap into the harness at the word of command and we make a flying start. They are just as keen to go as we are, and seem to enjoy it as well. I ride perhaps half a mile then jump off without stopping the team, and run ahead of the dogs up the long hill. I soon find my fur parka too heavy, and discard it for the lighter one made of drilling, in which I do the rest of my mushing to the end of the trail. Moccasins are on my feet, for the trail must be taken flat-footed if one is to have reasonable comfort.

After two or three miles we leave the broad road and strike the trail through the wilderness. Our sled is twenty-one inches wide, light and shod with steel, and the trail, henceforth, will be about twenty-four inches in width, sometimes sunken deep, where snow has not recently fallen and the trail has been well beaten, sometimes only a trace along the snow where the wind has blown it clean and where the trail is hard.

We soon begin to labor up the first divide. No more riding now. The trail is hard enough to dispense with snow-shoes, but heavy enough to make us both walk and labor. I strike the trail ahead, leaving Breeze to the handle-bars. I begin to feel the joy of it. The keen, light, dry air is like wine. The trail winds through the woods, along the edges of gorges, then up a steep mountain. Now the timber ceases and we have rounded, wind-swept summits. I leave the dogs far behind, for it is heavy pulling up the steep. Their bells tinkle faintly from below. I gain nearly a mile on them before they round the summit. I strike my lope down the farther side, but soon hear the bells as they charge down upon me and pass me, swinging on towards the roadhouse.

We only make twenty miles the first day, for it was nearly noon when we started, and we are glad to stop at "Bonanza Roadhouse" as dusk is coming on. How good the moose meat tastes! How sweet the beds of hard boards and blankets! The luxury of rest we enjoy to the full. The dogs are fed, our moccasins and socks hung up to dry, and we crawl in our bunks with sighs of relief. There is no floor in the roadhouse; all the lumber has been whipsawed by hand, the furniture manufactured out of boxes and stumps, the utensils of the rudest. But the luxury of splendid meat and good sour-dough bread and coffee makes us feel that we have all that goes to make life desirable.

An early morning start is necessary. We eat our breakfast by candle-light, fill up our thermos bottle with hot coffee, take a big hunk of roasted meat for lunch, and "hit the trail" by daylight. Twenty-six miles to-day—to

"Moorecreek Roadhouse." Snow begins to fall, and soon the trail is obliterated by the fast-coming feathery flakes. Now the snow-shoes must be unstrapped and one of us break the trail ahead. We take turns and swing along at a three and a half mile gait. This is real work, and we reach the roadhouse in the middle of the afternoon, but not so tired as on the preceding day.

These are samples of the journey throughout; but oh, the variety!—no two miles alike—and the panorama of beauty that unfolds before us!

"Each fir tree flings a bridal veil,
A bridal veil of shimmering white,
Like stately maidens tall and bright,
Slow marching as to solemn rite
Beside the ribbon of the trail."

Notice the beauty of the frost sparkling on the trees. The wonderful law that gives its own distinct varieties of frost crystals to each species of tree, fir, spruce, birch, cottonwood or alder, is exemplified so plainly here that, after the first examination, you can tell the kind of tree under the frost crystals by the shade of silver. The mountains tower above you, wind-swept, waving snow-banners. The vastness of that white hush awes and thrills you. A rough sound would be blasphemy in the solemn silence. The whole landscape is a poem.

To relate even the leading incidents of this "joy-mush" of three weeks would take up too much space. The longest distance we traveled in any one day was fifty-five miles; while our hardest and longest day's struggle through drifted snow and over a steep mountain pass yielded us only twelve miles of trail. In most of the roadhouses I found old friends, and, in several of them, Christian people who had been members of missions I had established in new mining camps. What grand times we had together! No fellowship is so warm and sweet as that of the wilderness. Of many adventures on the trail I can give but two.

One morning, about half-way from Iditarod to Seward, we left the fine cabin of French Joe, on the South Fork of the Kuskoquim River, under the two beautiful peaks, Mts. Egypt and Pyramid. We were making for Rainy Pass over the Alaskan Range. What follows is an extract from an account I wrote at the time.

The day out from Joe's I meet with my first disaster. We have nineteen miles of absolutely clear ice on the South Fork of the Kuskoquim. The river is full of air-holes and open riffles. The dogs swing along at a ripping pace, digging their toe nails into the hard ice, the sled slipping sideways and sliding dangerously near to the open places. Breeze often has to run ahead at full speed to choose a route, for there is no trail on the ice. Half-way up the river I "get gay," as Breeze calls it. I leave the handle-bars to find a route, and fall down hard on the smooth ice. A sharp pang strikes through the small of my back as if from a spear-thrust. I get up and go along, thinking the pain will cease, but soon I realize that I am in the grip of an old enemy, lumbago.

From this point on to Seward I cannot make a move without pain, sometimes so great that I gasp for breath. At night in the roadhouse I have great trouble in getting into my bunk, and sometimes Breeze has to lift me out in the morning. Were I at home I would be in bed for a couple of weeks with doctors and nurses fussing over me, but it is just as well that I cannot stop. I take the philosophy of an old fellow in the "Rainy Pass Roadhouse" near the summit of the range, who says the best cure for a lame back is to "keep on a- mushin'"!

Beyond Rainy Pass we drop into the canyon of Happy River, and here we have our famous moose-hunt. Soon after we enter the gorge we come upon its tracks—a big bull-moose. We have already traveled nearly thirty miles to-day, and are anxious to make the roadhouse twelve or fifteen miles further on; and now, here comes this big, blundering beast to poke our trail full of deep holes and excite our dogs. He is running ahead of us. The snow is five or six feet deep and he goes in almost to his back at every step. The walls of the canyon are sheer and he cannot escape up its side. The river turns and winds, and here and there are little patches of level ground, thick with large spruce trees.

For three miles we do not catch sight of the moose, but our dogs show that he is on ahead. In spite of my lame back I have to struggle on in front of them and bat "Leader" in the face with my cap, Breeze standing on the brake to keep them from running away. The moose tracks fill our trail for a while, smashing it all to pieces, then veer sideways to a little patch of woods, and the dogs go pell-mell in the moose track, burying our sled out of sight in the deep snow. Then we have to haul them around and lift the sled on the track again, and try to get them along the trail.

Three miles down the river we catch sight of the big moose, and the dogs go wild. "Sheep," who has been disposed to malinger, is the worst of the lot. He forgets all his maladies and weariness and dashes forward, but "Leader" will not leave the track and swings along as best he can, except when the moose is in full sight. Then I have to bat him in the face to keep the team in bounds. Our bells are tingling, our dogs barking and we are shouting. It is a fearsome thing to the bull-moose, this animated machine that is charging down the river at him. So on he struggles through the deep snow, spoiling our trail and filling my companion's mind with blasphemous thoughts which occasionally break out in expression, in spite of his respect for my "cloth."

Four miles of this moose-hunt, with the big brute growing more tired and we more anxious to pass him. Instead of our hunting the moose he is haunting us. At last, around a little point of woods, we see him lying down in the middle of the river right ahead of us. The dogs break bounds and almost upset me as they dash down the trail with Breeze standing on the brake and yelling "Whoa!" The weary bull-moose staggers to his feet again and makes the edge of the woods, but there lies down again.

The trail veers right up to him. I run ahead and take "Leader" and "Ring," one in each hand, and Breeze does the same with "Teddy" and "Sheep." "Moose" is more tractable and we can control him with our voices. We drag the dogs bodily with the sled behind, pass the big brute, his long face not a rod from us, and then, setting "Leader" on the trail again, we urge them down five miles further to "Happy River Roadhouse." That was *one* hunt in which I was glad to lose the game.

Four hundred miles from our starting point we put up at the "Pioneer Roadhouse" in the little town of Knik at the head of Cook's Inlet. This was one of half a dozen small towns around Knik Arm and Turn-again Arm, the two prongs of Cook's Inlet. These towns had been in existence for fifteen or twenty years, with gold-miners and their families living there; and yet, here at Knik, I preached the first sermon that had ever been preached in a region larger than the state of Pennsylvania! This visit led to the establishment of a number of missions in that region, which is now traversed by the new Government railroad. The towns of Anchorage and Matanuska have sprung into existence and a thriving population of railroad builders, coal miners, gold miners, farmers and men of other trades and professions has settled there.

I left Iditarod on March fifth. I swung into Seward at nine o'clock on the morning of March twenty-eighth and was heartily greeted and entertained by Rev. L. S. Pedersen, pastor of the Methodist Church. He was a photographer as well as a preacher, and took the picture of my arrival. In spite of their hard work, my dogs were fatter and fuller of "pep" than when we started.

I fairly cried when I bade my team good-bye at Seward, taking each beautiful head in my arms and talking to them all. They seemed to feel the parting as keenly as I, for there was a general chorus of mournful howls as I turned away. I never saw my splendid dogs again, for the man who engaged to take them back to Iditarod failed to keep to his bargain, and I had to give them to the man who cared for and fed them at Susitna. I shall never find another team like them.

Notwithstanding the heaviness of the trail, the bitter struggles over mountains and through deep snows, not to mention the pains of lumbago, I look back upon that trip and other trips like it with joyful recollection and longing to repeat the experience. I would rather take a trip through that beautiful wilderness, with my dogs, than travel luxuriously around the world on palatial steamboats. There is more fun in dog-mushing.

V

LOUIE PAUL AND THE HOOTZ

"OH, 'e's bad feller, dat hootz," exclaimed Louie Paul, our half-breed Stickeen young man, the blood of his French father sparkling in his eyes and gesturing in his hands and shoulders. "'E's devil, 'im. Dat's no swear—dat's truf. Bad spirit got him, sure. *Quonsum sallix* (Always mad). 'E no savvy scare, no savvy love, no savvy die. 'E's devil, dat's all."

Louie's handsome face and coal-black eyes were alive with excitement, as he danced about his big bundle of *tseek* (black bear) skins, which he had just brought into Stevens' store at Fort Wrangell, and was unwrapping, preparatory to bartering. His outburst of language was called out by a question of mine. I had been noticing with surprise that among the great numbers of black bear skins that were being brought into the Wrangell stores daily by the Indians, were none of the big brown bear—the *hootz*. I knew these brown bears to be very plentiful up the Stickeen and Iskoot Rivers where Louie had been hunting. At this season (it was in early May) both species of bears, having wakened from their long winter's sleep, were roaming the banks of the streams restlessly day and night, making up in their fierce activity for their six months of torpor. Their coats were at their best— long, silky, glistening, thick and soft. The skins of the black bear Louie had brought were prime. They were more than black. Their ebony surfaces shone and sparkled, beneath our handling, like black diamonds.

Fort Wrangell, Alaska, on Etolin Harbor

To the left may be seen the first Protestant Church in Alaska, built by Dr. Young, 1879

I knew that the skins of the hootz would be equally beautiful and twice as large as those of the tseek. They would not be tawny at this season, but a rich, velvety brown, the color of the Irish setter's coat. In my canoe trips and steamboat voyages up the Stickeen I had seen more brown bears than black, standing boldly out on the bank to watch the sputtering steamboat, or grubbing for roots and worms in the green patches up the mountain slopes.

"Why don't you shoot the big bears?" I asked Louie. "I saw four in a bunch the other day. Don't you see any in your hunting trips?"

"Oh, yes," he confessed, "me plenty see hootz. All time me see heem. Yestaday me see tree—big fellers; stand up, all same man."

"What's the matter, then?" I pressed him. "Are you afraid of them?"

"Yes, you bet you boots, I scare of heem. I no shame scare about hootz. S'pose I big fool, I no scare; I shoot heem.—You never see me again no mo'."

Louie Paul had two claims to special distinction. First, he was a very expert and successful bear hunter; and, second, he was the husband of the star pupil of Mrs. McFarland's Home for Girls,—Tilly, the handsomest and brightest of the girls whom we had rescued from the vileness, squalor and sin of heathen life, and were training to be examples and teachers of Christian civilization to their tribe.

I had taken Louie and Tilly the preceding fall and established them at Tongas, one hundred miles south of Wrangell, outfitting Tilly with school books, Bibles, Sunday-school supplies, etc., and paying her a salary as teacher to that wild tribe. Louie's task was to keep up the fires for the school, and to cook for his wife and supply her needs. He had stayed at home faithfully during the winter, procuring the venison, ducks, geese, fish, clams, crabs, and other articles of food they needed, and making himself useful around the branch mission, even occasionally leading in prayer, and exhorting the people. But the trapper's "call of the wild" sounded in the early spring—a call he could not resist. So here he was, having left Tilly to cook her own meals and make her own fires, while he explored the streams, bayous and lakes in his small canoe, pursuing the elusive plantigrades.

The natives of Alaska at that time were handicapped in their hunting by an order of the Government which forbade the Indians to own or use breech-loading guns. This order was enforced among our peaceful Alaska natives, who had never had a serious trouble with the whites, while the Sioux, Apaches and Nez Perces, who were often on the war-path, had all the Winchester, Henry and Enfield rifles they wanted.

The natives of Alaska at that time—the early eighties—had only breech-loading, smooth-bore Hudson Bay muskets; and their round bullets had not much penetrating power. They were all right for deer, but you might fill a hootz full of those big, round balls and he would still have strength to tear you to pieces.

"The more you pester them big bear with them old-fashioned smooth-bores," said one of the old white hunters at Fort Wrangell, "the madder he gits."

Louie Paul looked so much more like a white man than like an Indian, and talked English so fluently, that I had persuaded the collector of customs—the only civil officer we had in that region—to permit me to lend Louie my new 45-75 Winchester repeating rifle. The repeater was a hard-shooting, accurate gun, chambering twelve cartridges in the magazine—the most efficient rifle made at that time. Louie was a fine shot, and the possession of this rifle gave him a great superiority over all the other Indian bear-hunters. He made more money in his three or four weeks of hunting in the spring than Tilly earned by her winter's teaching.

"I should think you would not be afraid of a brown bear when you have my Winchester," I urged. "You could put half a dozen balls clean through him before he could get to you."

Louie shook his curly head doubtfully. "Mebby so; mebby not."

Then his face lit up with a broad grin. "Mebby so I be lak Buck. You hear about Buck an' Kokaekish?"

"No," I replied, scenting a story. "What about them?"

I knew both these men. Kokaekish was a fine old Indian, the father of one of our best boys, whose Christian name was Louis Kellogg, but whose Indian name was Kokaek. The name, Kokaekish, means "Kokaek's Father," illustrating the curious custom of the Thlingets of naming parents after their children.

"Buck" was a French Canadian, Alex Choquette—a white man who had married a Stickeen woman and had been adopted into the tribe. He had seemingly become in heart and life an Indian, talking the language of his tribe, thinking their thoughts and pursuing their customs. How thoroughly he had become Indianized was evidenced by the language of Shustaak—the old heathen chief who had adopted Buck. "Wuck," he said, "delate siwash. Yacka tolo konaway nesika kopa klemenhoot." (Buck is a genuine Indian. He can beat all the rest of us lying.)

True to this definition of him, Buck had built his log house—a combined dwelling-house, hotel and store—thirty miles up the Stickeen River, opposite the Great Glacier, right on the boundary line between Alaska and British Columbia. Here he sold blankets, guns, groceries and whiskey to the white miners and to the Indians. When the Canadian authorities attempted to arrest him for his illicit traffic he claimed to be on the American side. When the Alaska custom officers went after him, he was a Canadian. Thus for years he had carried on his crooked business and escaped punishment.

"You know Buck," Louie began, "he worse siwash dan anybody; but he alltam make fun odder Injun. One day Kokaekish come Buck store, buy powder.

"'Where you come?' Buck say.

"'Iskoot,' say Kokaekish, 'make dry dog salmon. Now too many hootz, me come back.'

"Buck laugh. 'Eehya-a-ah! You *shawat-too* (woman-heart); you coward! What for you 'fraid hootz? S'pose me, I shootem all.' Buck much laugh.

"Kokaekish, he shame. He head hang down, so. Buck more laugh. Bimeby Kokaekish say, 'Buck, you strong heart. You want killem hootz?'

"Buck big bluff. 'Sure' he say. 'You show me hootz, me shootem quick.' "'All

light, come along. Me showem you hootz now.' Kokaekish go he canoe.

"Buck shame for back out. He get Winchester, all same you rifle. 'Where you go?'

"'No far. Ict tintin, nesika clap.' (One hour, we find.)

"Dey go up Iskoot, mebby tree mile. Fin' leetle stream. Plenty humpback an' dog salmon dere. Flap, flap, splash in shallow place. All roun' de grass all flat —plenty tail, fin, bone. Buck look. He scare, but shame go back. Leetle hill dere by de creek. Plenty bush. Kokaekish an' Buck go up; sit down; wait. Pitty soon sitkum polakly (half night—twilight), Kokaekish ketch Buck arm. Whisper, 'Hootz come.'

"Buck look. Bear all same house—delate hya-a-as! (very big), come down creek. Swing slow an' lazy. Go in water; slap out big salmon on bank pitty near two man; go an' eatem.

"Kokaekish whisper, 'Why you no shootem, Buck? You brave man! You much want killem hootz. Shootem quick!'

"Buck scare stiff. 'Sh-sh-sh! you ol' fool!' he say. He toof clap all same medicine-man rattle; water come out on he face; he shake like Cottonwood leaf.

"Kokaekish laugh. 'More hootz come,' he say. Nodder big bear come; growl, gr-r-r! go fishin'. Den she-bear an' two leetle feller come. Mamma ketch salmon; leetle bear play; run up-hill mos' on top man. Nodder bear come. *Six Hootz*; ketch salmon; scrap; one chase nodder; play.

"Buck not quite die. He lie flat down. He's finger count he's bead; he play Maly; he shake.

"Kokaekish much laugh. He rub it in. 'You brave man, Buck. You white man —no scare nuttin'. You want see hootz. Me fin' heem. Why you no shootem?'

"Bimeby delate polakly (quite dark). All hootz go leetle way up creek. Kokaekish shake Buck. 'Mebby so, you no want more hootz, we go now.' Dey walk han' an' foot—all same dog. Buck fo'get he's rifle. Dey fin' canoe; paddle quick Buck house.

"Now all Injun put shame on Buck face. 'Hey, Buck, you want shootem hootz? You white man; you brave; no scare nuttin'. How many hootz you kill?' Buck delate shame. Mos' keel hese'f. Mebby so, I lak dat."

"No, Louie," I replied when we had done laughing, "you are not like Buck. You would keep your nerve, and at least account for some of the brown bears."

"Well," he ventured doubtfully, "dis Winshesser mighty fine gun. I t'ink I try hootz nex' tam."

A week afterwards Louie came to my house in great excitement. He knocked repeatedly before I could get to the door.

"Mista Yuy," he almost shouted, "you come see my hootz skin. My firs'; my las' too."

I went with him to the store where several fine black bear skins were displayed to an admiring group of whites and natives. With them was an enormous brown bear skin, the largest I had ever seen. The fur was beautiful —rich in color, thick and glossy; but it was bloody and badly mussed. Turning it over I saw that the skin was full of holes—fairly riddled. I counted seventeen perforations. The larger and more ragged of the holes marked the exit of the balls that had ranged clear through the bear.

"Why, Louie," I exclaimed, "what did you mean by spoiling this fine skin? It is like a sieve. You have taken away more than half its value by shooting it up like that."

Louie danced about like a monkey—head, hands, feet, his whole body gesturing, his voice rising higher and louder as he went on with his story.

"You lissen me! I see dis big feller stan' up all same man. Open place; no big tree. Maybe hunner ya'd. I say me, 'Louie, you betta draw good bead dis tam. You shoot heem straight troo de heart, keel heem dead fust shot.'

"I shoot; he fall down. Klosh tumtum (good heart), me. I put de gun on shoul'er. Den I look. I 'stonish. De hootz, he git up queek; he come straight fo' me. I shoot queek; he fall down; he git up; he come for me. I shoot; I shoot; I shoot; he fall down; he fall down; he git up; he come for me. You betcha boots I hit heem ev'y tam. I scare to miss. I forgit how many catridge. I shoot; I shoot; I say, 'Dat's de las'; now he git me; dat's de las'; now he git me.'

"I git awful scare. I t'ink, 'Tilly widow now fo' sure. Nobody git wood fo' her no mo'.'—Dat bear git close—right here! He jus' goin' grab me. I mos' fall down; I so scare. I try once mo'. I put my gun agains' he's head. I shoot; he fall down; he don' git up no mo'. My las' catridge. I put ten ball t'rough heem. *No-mo'-hootz-fo'-me!*"

VI

OLD SNOOK AND THE COW

IN the early missionary days at Fort Wrangell I had to be a little of everything to those grown-up, naughty, forest-wise but world-foolish children of the islands whom we called Thlingets and Hydas. I had to be carpenter, and show them how to build better houses. I had to be undertaker, and teach them to make coffins and bury their dead decently. I had to be farmer, showing them how to raise turnips, potatoes, cabbage and peas. Once I gave a package of turnip seed to an old Indian woman. Towards the close of the season I went to see her garden. I found that she had dug a big hole and put all the turnip seed in it. You can imagine the result.

Among other things, I had to be doctor and surgeon to those people. I had never taken a course at a medical school and knew very little about medicine or surgery. But I had books and studied them and did the best I could. The hardest surgical cases I had were the result of little love-taps by old Mr. Hootz, the big brown bear. This bear is almost identical, except in color, with *ursus horribilis*, the grizzly—he is as large and ferocious and as hard to kill. Farther west in Alaska he has the true grizzly color and is called the silver-tip; but in Southeastern Alaska he is a rich brown, the female being much lighter in color than the male.

Once the Indians brought to me a man who had been foolish enough to shoot a hootz with his smooth-bore musket. The bear charged on the Indian, gave him one tap with his paw and went away. The poor man presented a horrible appearance. One eye was torn out, the skin of one side of his face torn loose and hanging down on his shoulder, the cheek laid entirely open. I did my best for him, washed his awful wound, replaced the skin on his face and took many stitches; but I couldn't make a pretty man of him.

Another Indian was hunting in the spring when he came across a little brown cub, and thought he would have a fine pet. He had just caught the little fellow and was trying to hush its cries, when suddenly the mother-bear came on him like an avalanche and he was knocked senseless. When he came to, hours afterwards, he was unable to move. The bear had torn off much of his scalp with the first blow, and then had bitten and chewed him from head to foot, injuring his spine, so that he could never walk again. I dressed twenty-one wounds which the angry she-bear had given him.

But the greatest example of the strength and ferocity of the hootz of which I ever knew was afforded by the adventure of an Irishman—a gold-prospector, whom we called Big Mike. He was a giant in stature—over six feet, broad and stalwart, physically the king of the Cassiar miners. He was a good- natured, happy-go-lucky fellow, a typical gold-prospector, making money very fast at times and spending it just as fast. Like the most of the miners of the Cassiar region (which was reached by traveling by steamboat from Victoria to Fort Wrangell, then by canoe or river steamboat up the Stickeen River a hundred and fifty miles, then across country by pack-train from one hundred to two hundred miles, according to the location of the "diggings"), Mike made Fort Wrangell his stopping place to and from the Cassiar, sometimes wintering there.

One day Dave Flannery, another Irishman, whose Stickeen wife was a member of my mission, came hurriedly up to my house.

"I wish you'd come down and see Big Mike," he said; "he's hurrt bad."

I found Mike in one of the miners' shanties on the beach, lying on a bed, entirely helpless. He could only use his arms, his legs being paralyzed. This was the story he told me:

"Me an' me partner, Steve," he began, "has been prospectin' up the Iskoot." (A tributary of the Stickeen which runs into it about twenty-five miles from its mouth.) "Ye know the Iskoot—a domd bad river—little flat islands thick as spots on a burrd-dog—th' river swift an' shaller—lots av quick-sands an' rocks everywhere—th' shores an' th' islands all matted thick wid trays an' underbrush—big fallen trays lyin' across one anodher an' odher trays growin' out av thim—an' alders, willows, divil-clubs and salmon-berry bushes thicker'n hair on a cat.

"Well, me an' Steve set up our tint by a trickle av cold water in a side gulch, an' thought to spind th' sayson prospectin'. Th' thickets an' brush has scared off prospectors, an' it's new counthry. A wake ago Oi made up me pack for four or five days' prospectin'—blankets, fly tint, an' some grub, wid gold- pan, pick, shovel an' coffee-pot on top.

"Afther an hour o' harrd worrk Oi'd got mebby half a moil from camp, when Oi come to Sathan's own pile o' logs an' brush, stuck up ev'ry-which-way, wid bushes an' divil-clubs atween. Ye cuddn't see a yarrd. Oi tackled it as well as Oi cud wid me pack, an' got onto th' top log. Th' brush wuz that thick Oi cuddn't see pwhat wuz undher me. Oi tuk hold av a limb an' swung down into th' bushes. But before I touched th' groun'—gr-r-r—woof! somethin' of fur an' iron was all over an' aroun' me; me breath was squshed out o' me; somethin' was tearin' the cords out o' me neck an' shouldher, an' me back was bruk intoirly.

"Oi've some repitation as a sthrong man, an' Oi've niver met th' man Oi cuddent down in a fair wrassle; but this thing thut had me didn't play fair. He tuk a foul hold o' me when Oi wasn't lookin', an' niver guv me a chanst to break ut. Whin Oi swung down me left arrum wuz straight up, aholt av th' limb, an' the right wan wuz steadyin' me pack. Th' brute pinned that fast, an' Oi cud no more move it than a baby cud lift a ton.

"When Oi got me sinses gathered togither, an' knowed Oi wuz in the clutches av a bear, me dandher riz an' Oi thought av me knoif. 'Twas in a scabbard on me roight hip, an' that han' was hild toight agin me pack. Me blankets saved me ribs from bein' all stove in.

"Oi tried to twist aroun' an' git me knoif wid me lift han', but it was loik a mouse thryin' to pry off th' paws av a cat. Me fate wuz aff th' groun' an' Oi had no purchase. At las' Oi got ahold av th' handle av th' knoif. Jist as Oi felt me sinses lavin' me Oi got th' knoif an' begun to dig it wid all me strent into th' bear's belly, workin' upwards an' thryin' fer his heart. Thin ev'rythin' wint black.

"Whin Oi come to th' sun was hoigh. Ut must o' bin tree hours Oi laid there sinseless. Oi throied to git up, but me legs wuz dead. Oi cud pull mesilf up a little wid me arrms, an' there Oi saw fur th' furrst toim th' baste thut bruk me. He wuz lyin' besoid me, stone dead. 'Twas all th' joy Oi had.

"Well, there Oi wuz, undher all th' logs an' brush, an' down in a little hollow in th' muck—an' helpless. 'Twas too fur away to make Steve hear. Oi hollered as best Oi cud, but 'twas no use. Th' bear hadn't left me much breath. Then Oi thought Oi'd thry annyhow. Me arrums wuz good, an' th' bushes wuz thick, so Oi begun to pull meself along troo th' muck by me hands, usin' me knoif whin th' bushes blocked me. It tuck me two hours to gain th' top av th' hill in soight av th' camp, an' anither to make a flag av a bit o' ma shurrt an' wave it on a pole so that Steve cud see it. He drug me down to camp, put me in th' canoe, an' here Oi am wid all th' man squose out av me, bad cess to th' bear. Ef anny one says anny man c'n fight anny bear wid his two han's an' bate it, tell 'im from me he's a loiarr."

We raised a purse and sent Big Mike on the monthly steamboat to Victoria. He lived several years. They gave him the position of watchman on the wharves, and we used to see him—a pathetic figure, creeping slowly about the dock, first with a pair of crutches and then with a cane. He was never a man again, after his encounter with the hootz.

Native Houses, Showing Totem Poles

In such a house Snook lived

But although the hootz was so strong and so fierce there was in almost every Indian tribe one who would attack and kill him. In the Stickeen tribe this man's name was Snook. Tilly, our star pupil and my interpreter, proudly pointed him out, one day when I was down in the Indian village, as her granduncle and the head of the family.

I had never before seen Snook. He never came to church or to my house. He must have been sixty or sixty-five years old—a great, stalwart, big-boned savage with a huge head and a tremendous jaw. He was almost always absent from Fort Wrangell, hunting in the mountains or fishing among the islands. "My gran'fader, the greatest hootz-hunter in the world," was Tilly's introduction.

It was on the occasion of a visit with Tilly to the community house of her family. As she spoke she went behind the carved totemic corner post which supported the roof, and brought forth old Snook's most valuable and proudest possession. It was a beautiful spear. The shaft was of crabapple wood and eight feet long, thick enough for a good grip, and polished until it shone like brown granite. It was carved all over with the totemic images of the eagle and the brown bear, the totems of Snook's family. The head was made of a large steel rasp and was a foot and a half long, five inches across in the widest place, finely pointed, the edges sharp as a razor. The handle of the spear-head was let into the end of the shaft in a very ingenious way, and secured by many tightly wrapped turns of a cord of deer-sinew. It was a most perfect and ferocious weapon. I learned that the chief of another tribe had offered a slave, whose value was five hundred blankets, for the spear, and his offer had been refused.

All efforts to get Snook to talk about his hunting exploits were unavailing. He only grunted and went on with some carving with which he was occupied. But Sam Tahtain, a member of Snook's family, who was noted for his powers of oratory, described most graphically, in a mixture of Chinook, Thlinget and bad English, Snook's way of killing the big bears. He acted it so perfectly that even if I had not understood a word, the scene would have stood out very vividly before my mental vision. He showed the hootz grubbing among mossy logs and flirting the salmon out of a swift mountain stream; then Snook came in sight, creeping stealthily through the forest, a flintlock musket in one hand, his spear in the other. From that point the story grew more animated and the gestures more rapid to the climax. I can best tell it in the present tense:

The bear hears a stick snap and catches a faint human odor; he stands up on his hind feet to investigate. His lips are drawn back from his big teeth, and he snarls a question.

The man dodges behind a tree; creeps closer—cautiously flits from tree to tree—moves slowly out from a sheltering trunk—sinks on one knee—raises his gun—aims. "*Bang!*" from the gun,—"wah-a-ah-gr-r-r!" from the bear. The bear whirls round and round, biting his wound; then he charges straight for the man, his teeth champing, his jaws slavering.

The man throws away the gun and takes his spear in both hands. He steps boldly out in the open and stands still, his left foot advanced, his spear slanting upwards, braced for the shock. The bear comes galumphing on, his hair on end, his sideways strut showing his anger and his readiness for the battle.

When within a few feet of the man the bear stops short with a startling "Woof!" and stands upright on his hind feet. The man knows this habit of the hootz, and seizes the opportunity. He springs forward before the bear is steadied on his two feet and thrusts mightily with his spear. The bear strikes viciously at the man and howls hoarsely. A stream of red gushes out from the wide wound. Now the bear attacks, his fangs gleaming, his long claws standing stiffly out. He jumps and strikes and slashes with his teeth at the man.

The man is alert—firm and sure on his feet—quick as lightning, yet steady.

He dodges and leaps about the bear, feinting and thrusting. Again and again the spear goes home. The froth from the bear's jaws is bloody now, while the man's face is covered with drops of sweat. The breath of both comes in gasps. The air seems full of violent motion and raucous sounds. At every fresh wound the bear howls—"wa-a-ah"—this changes immediately to a vicious growl as he rears on his hind feet again and rushes to the fray. The man begins to shout his war-cry—"hoohooh—hoohooh"—as he jabs his terrible weapon into the bear's breast.

The bear is visibly weakening. His eyes grow dim, his rushes and blows have less steel and lightning in them. The man begins to taunt him, "Oh, you big-chief hootz—I thought you brave man—strong man. You no brave—no strong. You just like baby. Why you no stand up, fight like man?"

At last the bear, sick and faint with loss of blood, but game to the end, stands with paws outstretched, swaying like a drunken man. The man comes close, and, bending back to gain force for his blow, thrusts upward and forward with all his strength, striking just under the bear's breast bone and buries the spear-head, splitting the heart in two. Over on his back topples the great beast, his paws feebly twitching, his last breath bringing with it a great rush of blood.

The man, as soon as he can recover breath, puts his foot on the bear's neck, singing in quaint minor strain a brief song of triumph. Then he hastens to prop the bear's mouth open with a stick, to let his spirit go forth in peace, and he also places between the dying jaws a piece of dried salmon, that the bear may not lack food when he goes to join the *hoots-kwany*—the bear-people, in that spirit land of forests and mountains to which all brown bears, good and bad, must go.

Sam Tahtain was a little man, in striking contrast with his giant brother, Snook, but he entered into his recital with infinite energy, dancing about the floor, striking and thrusting, acting the bear's part and then the man's, shouting and growling out his words; and when he had finished, his own face was bathed in perspiration. His acting was an artless piece of art, very perfect in its way; and it certainly thrilled the Indians who had drawn around in an eager circle as the recitation proceeded, their fervent indrawn exclamations of wonder and admiration supplying the most genuine applause.

But I must confess that the antics of the little man, and his evident pride in his own performance, struck me as irresistibly funny; and I could not help recalling a verse I had learned when a boy:

> "Little man with the wild, wildeye,
> Man with the long, long hair,
> Why do you dance about the floor?

Why do you beat the air?
Why do you howl and mutter so?
Why do you shake your fist?"
Said the little man, in a deep, deep voice,
"I'm an el-o-cu-tion-ist!"

But the Indians saw nothing funny in Sam's oratory—it thrilled them through and through. Even old Snook, the hero of the story, ceased his carving, fixing his eyes intently on the speaker, and rewarding him with a fervent "*Kluh-yukeh!*" To exactly translate that exclamation will require a paraphrase—"My, but that was good!"

But Tilly thought only of the glory of her granduncle. Her eyes shone with pride, and she whispered to me, "Isn't my gran'fader, Snook, just the bravest man you ever heard of? Why, he isn't afraid of anything."

The other Indians also yielded Snook the palm for courage and strength. They looked upon him as a sort of Indian superman, lauding him in their speeches, and being careful not to offend him. He was the hero of the Stickeens.

And, indeed, I was much of the same opinion. Certainly a man who would stand up, single-handed, to a grizzly and kill him with a spear, must have unqualified nerve and courage. Surely nothing on earth could frighten a mighty bear-hunter like that.

Well, listen. A few days after this visit to Snook's house I was sitting in my house, which was within the stockade of the old fort. The posts of this stockade, some twelve feet high and firmly spiked together, had been put in place about sixteen years before, when the fort was first established. Although many of the posts were rotting, the circle enclosing the parade ground, barracks, hospital and officers' quarters was still unbroken. Our house was one of the old officers' dwellings and not far from the gateway which led "up the beach" towards the Indian village of temporary houses in which the "foreign Indians"—those from distant tribes—encamped. On the other side of the fort another gateway led "down the beach," through the town with its stores and white man's houses, to the large community houses of the Stickeens. To go from one Indian town to the other you had to pass through the fort.

It was a lovely, sunny day in midsummer. Everything was peaceful about the old fort. School was in session in the old hospital, our little children were playing on the grass, and our old cow, "Spot," was feeding in the gateway.

This cow was a little black and white Holstein which the ladies of Pennsylvania had purchased for Mrs. Young's training-school, and to supply our babies and the native babies with fresh milk. She was the first cow which had been brought to Fort Wrangell, and was a great curiosity and wonder to the Indians. The Thlingets had no name for cattle, because these animals were not known in Alaska; so they adopted the Chinook name—moosmoos—and, owing to the Thlingets' inability to pronounce any consonant that brings the lips together, they called it "wusoos."

Our little "wusoos" was gentle and tame as a kitten. Our children used to hang onto her tail, and feed her bunches of grass and leaves of cabbage. Once I came upon a group that made me laugh. "Spot" was lying down and placidly chewing her cud; Abby, aged five, was seated between the cow's horns; while Alaska (Lassie), who was three, with her little dog, Jettie, in her arms, was sprawling on Spot's back.

This peaceful summer's morning the cow was cropping the grass by the gate. Suddenly the silence was shattered by a strong Indian voice, pitched high through fear, calling to me: "*Uh-eedydashee; uh-eedydashee, uh-Ankow; uh-eedydashee!*" (Help me; help me, my chief; help me!)

I ran quickly out of the house and through the gateway in the direction of the cries, which were growing more agonizing. I thought somebody was being murdered. I rushed past "Spot," who was calmly munching grass, undisturbed by the hullabaloo. At first I could see nobody; then I discovered the huge bulk of old Snook, the hootz-hunter, crouching behind a stump. His face was as pale as its coating of smoke and grease would permit, and he was shaking like a leaf.

"Why, Snook!" I cried in Thlinget, "what's the matter? Is anything wrong in the Indian village?"

He pointed a trembling finger towards the cow and quavered, "Drive that thing away!"

The thought of that famous old bear-hunter, scared to death at my gentle old cow, was too much for me, and I burst into a roar of laughter. When I had recovered my powers of speech and locomotion I walked to "Spot" and put my arm over her neck.

"This is a *shawat wusoos*" (a woman cow), I explained. "She will not hurt anybody. See how kind and gentle she is."

Snook was unconvinced. His eyes were fixed in fascinated terror upon "Spot," and he dodged at every motion of her head.

"Eehya-a-ah!" he answered in contempt, "she knows white man; she doesn't know Indian. See the sharp horns on her head!" and he refused to come away from the shelter of the stump until I had driven "Spot" away some distance; and even then he sidled past, eyeing her apprehensively and then hurrying through the gateway and across the parade ground with the air of one who has escaped deadly peril.

The memory of Snook and the cow has often braced me up when I was tempted to retreat from the path of duty, because I did not know what was in the gateway, or because of unfamiliar obstacles. It is the unknown that terrifies us. If we march right up to the bugaboos that stand across our way, we will find the terrible horned monster change into something no more harmful than a gentle old cow.

VII

NINA AND THE BEARS

ALL these stories are true, in their essential points. In some of them, however, I have to change or suppress the names of persons and towns, because the characters introduced are still living, and might not like publicity. That is the case in this story.

Ever since the great gold stampede of 1897 into the Klondike, it has been my duty, as it certainly has been my pleasure, to follow the new gold stampedes into different parts of Alaska, and be at the beginning of most of the new gold camps and towns of the great Territory of the Northwest. Of course I began preaching as soon as I arrived at one of these camps, holding my first services on log piles, under the trees, in tents or saloons or lodging houses—wherever I could gather together a congregation.

Always, the next thing was to start a Sunday-school, if there were any children in the camp, or at least a Bible class, if there were only grown people. I always had hymn-books and a baby-organ along, and was sure of finding people to play the organ and sing. The gold-seekers are not all roughs and toughs, as some people think, but just such people as may be seen in the States, and a large proportion of them are Christians.

One of the greatest of these gold stampedes occurred in the heart of Alaska—in the center of a great wilderness until then unexplored. A rich vein of gold was struck deep down in the frozen ground. The news spread, and soon thousands of eager gold-seekers from all parts of Alaska, from the Pacific States, from Canada, and later from all parts of the United States came over the mountains from the coast, down the Yukon from Dawson City, up the Yukon from Nome and from other directions; traveling by steamboat, poling boat and canoe on the rivers, and with dog-sled, horse-sled and hand-sled in the winter over the mountains, and with packs on their backs and guns in their hands in the summer.

Of course I was with the crowd. I never liked to miss the fun of a great scramble like that. When I got to the big new camp I set up my tent and began to prepare a preaching-place and to advertise a meeting for the next Sunday by putting up posters on stumps and trees. I also called the children to come and be organized into a Sunday-school. About twenty children came the first Sunday.

Among them was a pretty little Swedish girl, named Nina. She had blue eyes, flaxen hair and rosy cheeks, and was about twelve years old. She won my heart at once, and soon we were great chums. She was so bright and pleasant and sweet, and such a fearless and intelligent outdoor girl, that one could not help loving her. She was always at Sunday-school and church, always knew her lessons, and sang so heartily and tunefully that people turned their heads to see her, and her sunny smile drew answering smiles even from care-worn faces.

I soon found that among Nina's accomplishments she was already a good shot with both rifle and shotgun; and when the snow began to fall in October I took her with me on a couple of rabbit-hunts, and her glee at getting the biggest bag of snow-shoe rabbits was very enjoyable. Rabbits formed our principal meat-supply that winter.

When the cold weather of November covered the rivers, creeks and lakes with ice and carpeted the hills and valleys with snow, a big stampede occurred away from the town of log houses into which the camp of tents had grown. Almost every one who had a dog-team and sled packed up an outfit of food, blankets, tent and sheet-iron stove, and "mushed" away into the mountains, prospecting for gold. If no dogs were available, two men, or sometimes a man and his wife, would harness themselves to a sled with their outfit aboard, and, depending upon their guns for their meat supply, would cheerily set forth into the trackless wild, following the water-courses until they found a likely- looking creek, when they would halt and build a snug log cabin, and spend the winter prospecting. To those who had courage, some knowledge of woodcraft and love of nature, this adventurous life was very enticing. Thousands of men in Alaska, to this day, spend their summers in the towns, working at their trades or professions, and then, on the approach of winter, invest the money they have earned in an outfit of provisions, tools and ammunition, and bury themselves in the wilderness again. It is a great life; and I have often felt strongly tempted to leave everything and join these brave spirits for a winter's stay in the McKinley range of mountains.

One day, about the middle of November of that year, little Nina came into our house and threw herself into our arms, crying as if her heart would break.

"Why, Nina dear," asked my wife, "what is the matter? Is any one sick or dead?"

"Oh, no," she sobbed, "but I can't come to Sunday-school any more. Papa and Mamma and I are going away off into the mountains to-morrow, and we'll never come back here again."

We petted and soothed her, the best comfort I could give her being the thought of the great hunting adventures that were before her. So the wilderness swallowed up my brave little friend, and for eight years I had no word of her. By that time I was at another large gold camp, in a distant part of the great Yukon Valley.

I was the only minister in a region larger than Pennsylvania. My parish extended from two to five hundred miles in different directions from the camp in which I wintered. That winter I traveled with my dogs between two and three thousand miles, in preaching and exploring trips. Magazines, papers and books sent me by churches, Sunday-schools, Boys' Scouts, and women's missionary societies, I found three hundred miles from my central reading room, in miners' and trappers' cabins and in roadhouses to which I had sent them.

About the middle of the winter I was delighted to get a letter from Nina. It was written from a point about two hundred and fifty miles distant, in that great game-stocked region which lies west of the Alaska Range, of which Mt. McKinley, "The Top of the Continent," is the highest peak. It was a cheery, girlish letter—just such an one as I might have expected from Nina—grown-up. It told me of her marriage, two years before, to a young man whom I had known—one who had loved her when she was a little girl, had followed her and her parents to the western wilderness, waited patiently for her to grow up, and, now that they were married, seemed to her all that was admirable and complete in manhood. It was her one romance and was very sweet and perfect.

Nina and her husband were living in a large cabin on one of the trails that led from the Interior to the Coast. Nina called it a roadhouse, and, though low and dark, with only poles for floor, and pole-bunks for beds, it was fitted for the accommodation of a dozen travelers. Nina was queen of a wide realm. Her cabin was a hundred and twenty-five miles from that of the nearest white woman. They were two hundred miles from the nearest store. They were in the heart of the richest game region of North America—the western foot-hills of the Alaska Range. They were prospectors for gold in the summer; farmers, raising their own potatoes and vegetables and wheat for their chickens; trappers during the winter; hunters all the time; and hotel-keepers during the six months when snow and frozen streams and lakes lured travelers along the lonely trail.

There was in Nina's letter, however, no hint of loneliness; rather a joyful tone of contentment, as one of God's favored creatures; and of comradeship with the things about her—the mountains, the forests and the myriads of animals, small and great. She invited me to come and make them a long visit and have a big hunt. Her letter also spoke of the one need in her life that I could supply—Bibles, books and magazines.

Very few travelers came my way who had passed Nina's that winter, but from most of them I heard of my little chum, and always in terms of enthusiastic praise.

"I am a city man," said a young lawyer from Seattle, "and am in this wild land just long enough to make my stake and get back to the rattle of the street- cars. The 'call of the wild' has no allurement for me. There is just one thing that could make me settle down in Alaska, and that is to find such a mate as that little woman."

"Know her?" repeated a rugged, black-eyed man of thirty whom I had met on the Chilcoot Pass in '97. "Who doesn't? Say; she's a great woman. Why, I'd go out of my way a hundred miles, any time, just to see her smile, and to taste her grouse-pie or roast sheep. Tell you what she did this last trip: As I swung into the edge of their clearin' a pair of sharp-tailed grouse flew up to the top of a dry spruce, a hundred yards from the cabin. Nina was complainin' that she had no makin's of grouse pie in the house, knowin' my likin' for the same. I told her about the two I'd scared up. 'Lend me a shotgun,' I said, 'and I'll go back and try for a shot at them.' We stepped to the door for a look. There set the two grouse on the spruce, lookin' like robins agin the sky. Nina took down a twenty-two rifle from the wall and put some 'extra-long' shells in the magazine. I thought she was goin' to give the gun to me, and I planned to sneak back till I got under the birds before riskin' a shot; but she stood in the doorway and swung the rifle up quick and easy. Crack, crack! and dogged if them chickens didn't come tumblin' right down. I never seen such shootin'. Then she slipped on her snow-shoes and went and got the grouse and made me my pie. She's sure a little bit of 'all right.'"

I asked him if he had seen the magazines and Bibles I had sent her. With a sheepish grin he took out of his pocket a little red Testament, and handed it to me. I saw his name on the fly-leaf with her initials under it.

"First I've carried since I was a kid," he confessed. "And she made me promise to *read* it! A woman that can be a bright little Christian in a place like that, and a dead game sport, too, can make me do most anything. Joe [Nina's husband] is a lucky guy."

Naturally such reports as these made me all the more anxious to see this queen of the wilderness again. The necessity of taking a seven-hundred-mile trip to the Coast in March gave me the opportunity.

Oh, boys, you'll never know the real joy of living till you take a winter trip with dog-sled in Alaska. The keen, fine air, lung-filling, invigorating; your dogs yelping with eagerness, their feet twinkling, the sled screaming its delight; frost-diamonds sparkling from every branch, frost-symphonies played by the ice-harps under your feet; your own struggle, achievement, triumph, against and over the cold, the difficulties of the trail, the long miles.

"The morning breaks, the stars grow pale,
Your huskies leap, shrill shrieks the sled;
You follow free with flying tread;
A joy to live! What joy! to thread
The fluted ribbon of the trail."

It was near the sunset of a beautiful, bright day that I swung into Joe's clearing. For three days I had been headed almost directly towards Dinali— The Great One, and Dinah's Wife (Mt. McKinley and Mt. Foraker). Higher and higher these majestic mountains heaved their mighty shoulders. The country became more broken and rugged. Lesser mountains raised their white heads all around me. Only a few inches of snow covered the ground instead of the six to ten feet that prevailed farther west. The character of the trees had changed—more birch, cottonwood and other deciduous timber; less tamarack, hemlock and swamp spruce.

Signs of abundant life were everywhere. Fox, wolf, lynx and wolverine tracks criss-crossed the snow in all directions; great moose tracks going in a straight line, and the imprint of thousands of caribou hoofs crossing and obliterating each other, but keeping in the same general direction showed the presence of abundance of big game; while grouse, ptarmigan and rabbit tracks were so numerous that my dogs were kept excited and on the "keen jump" every minute.

On the bank of a small river, in a clearing of a couple of acres cut out of a forest of great fir and cedar trees, stood Joe's log-cabin roadhouse. Enough of the big trees had been left standing to shade the house. In front of it were a dozen cozy log dog-kennels, and behind it was a garden enclosed in a picket and wire fence.

As soon as "Leader's" bells gave shrill notice of my arrival the door flew open, a bright little figure in gingham and moccasins, with yellow hair flying and blue eyes sparkling, rushed at me, and I received the first good hug that I had experienced since leaving my wife and daughters in the East a year before.

A cheery voice cried, "Oh, you dear old man, you. I've been watching for you every day for two weeks. I was so afraid you weren't coming!"

Joe's welcome, though not so demonstrative, was none the less hearty. It was worth dog-mushing two hundred and fifty miles to have such a reception. As soon as I stepped into the house I was made keenly aware that I was in the home of hunters and trappers. In all my wide experience of wilderness homes I had never seen one like this. The long, low cabin had two rooms. The smaller was kitchen and dining-room, having a sheet-iron range and home-made tables, shelves and chairs. The larger room had a good sized sheet-iron heating stove in the center, and was almost filled with bunks in tiers of three each, built in double rows the length of the room. A little chamber enclosed with snowy caribou buck-skin, the skins sewn together most skillfully with sinew thread, was Nina's bedroom. The poles which formed the floors had been hewn and laid so carefully that they looked like boards. The tables and shelves were of whipsawed lumber, every article showing painstaking skill.

"Joe and I made the cabin and everything in and about it, all ourselves," Nina boasted.

"What!" I exclaimed, "you two rolled up these heavy logs, without any help?"

"Yes, indeed. We used block-and-tackle. It isn't so hard when you know how; and it was great fun."

"But the lumber for the doors and tables and window-sash—it's so true and smooth and beautiful; how did you get that?" I asked.

"Whipsawed and hand-planed it all," she replied. "You see, we came here two years ago this month, just after we were married. The Government was surveying this trail, and we thought we'd build this roadhouse and pick up a few dollars taking care of travelers. But chiefly we chose this place because it was so beautiful and such a game country. Then it has never been prospected for gold.

"Joe and I each had a good dog-team and sled when we were married. We loaded the sleds with tools, hardware, stoves and dishes, glass for the windows, some flour, sugar, beans and a few other groceries, and brought our traps and plenty of ammunition for our guns. It was hard breaking trail through the deep snow on the east side of the Alaska Range, but nice going on this side. We mushed the two hundred and fifty miles from the coast in two weeks; and had some time for trapping before warm weather."

"How do you get 'outside' in the summer time?" I inquired.

"We can't, and we don't need to. We spent that first summer building this house, making garden, gathering berries, drying fish, hunting and getting ready for the winter. Almost all our wants are supplied right here. From the middle of April till the middle of October we don't see a human being, except now and then an Indian, or a stray prospector."

"What a lonesome life!" I exclaimed.

"Now, Doctor, I know you don't mean that," protested Nina. "Why, this is the most companionable place in the world. It is full of friendly creatures. The winter before I was married I spent three months in San Francisco. I nearly died, I was so lonely and homesick. I'd meet thousands of people on the streets every day, and not get a word or smile from one of them. I wouldn't give my little 'Red' for the whole crowd."

"Who's Red?" I asked.

Nina leaned forward and made a squeaking noise with her lips. Instantly a little furry creature of a bright scarlet color, with a short tail, jumped out of a box in the corner, ran to her and up her hand and arm to her shoulder and then down to her knee, where he stood stiffly erect like a soldier at attention. He was so quick and comical in his motions and so full of tricks that he kept us laughing.

"I had three Reds," explained Nina, "but a weasel got two of them before I got the weasel. I have had many other pets besides the wood-mice. There isn't a creature in all the forest that would do me harm unless I hurt it first. And I don't have a grudge against any of them, except the hawks and owls that come after my chickens."

The most striking feature about the cabin, however, was the abundance and variety of furs and other trophies of the chase. Adorning and almost covering one end of the room was an enormous moose head. At the other end was a wonderful caribou head. Over the windows were beautiful heads of the white mountain sheep, the bighorn of the Northwest.

But the pelts! Great bunches of mink, marten, fisher, otter, muskrat and beaver; scores of red fox, with here and there a priceless black or silver fox; lynx, wolf, wolverine and black bear.

"We have four lines of traps, each five miles long," explained Nina; "and Joe and I each take two lines every other day, spending the alternate days caring for the skins. We are making bear traps now, getting ready for Bruin when he comes out of his den. We have about four thousand dollars' worth of furs caught this winter, and we'll make it five before warm weather."

But the most imposing objects of all in the cabin were two tremendous rugs—the skins of the *ursus gigas* or Kodiak bear—the largest of existing carnivorous mammals. Joe had learned something of taxidermy, and the heads were nicely preserved, the big teeth and claws showing, the skins being lined with red blankets. The largest of these rugs was over twelve feet long, the distance from nose to tail over ten feet, the lateral spread being almost as great. The fur was a rich brown in color, deep, thick and soft.

At my exclamation of wonder and admiration, Joe began eagerly to tell me the story of the rugs; but his wife stopped him.

"Better wait till after supper, Joe," she said.

Ah, that supper! The supreme physical pleasure of it lingers in my memory still. Moose soup with potatoes, turnips, carrots and onions from their garden in it; fresh grayling, caught in the fall and frozen; ruffed grouse pie; roast mountain sheep—the best meat that grows; omelet made of eggs laid that day; moose-nose cheese, delicately pickled; fine sour-dough bread with raspberry jam and currant jelly; pie made of fresh blueberries, the berries having been picked in the fall and preserved by the simple process of pouring water on them and letting them freeze. All of these viands, except the bread, being the products of Nina's labor or marksmanship, made them doubly sweet. Where else in the world could you get a meal like that—or the appetite to devour it all?

"Well," began Joe, when, sated, I lay back in the easy-chair curiously fashioned of moose horns, while the young couple washed the dishes, "I'm mighty proud of them rugs. They're Nina's, both of 'em, and I reckon there's no other girl in the world would of tackled the job she did, and got away with it. It scares me every time I think of it, and I don't know whether I'd oughter scold her or pet her up."

"Nonsense!" protested his wife; "you know you'd have done exactly as I did if you'd been here."

"Maybe I would," he retorted, "but I wouldn't of let *you* take that risk."

Five Kodiak Bears

The bear to the right is twice the size of a Grizzly

"It was the first of last November," he resumed. "I'd taken the two sleds and all the dogs, as soon as I thought the ice was strong enough, and I'd gone two hundred miles to the store at Ophir to lay in our winter's outfit. The ice towards the coast wasn't strong enough to make safe mushin', and Nina was all alone here for more'n three weeks. I knowed she would make the reg'lar round of the traps and keep things goin' just as usual. She's never learned to be afraid—that girl.

"Well, one mornin' she was gettin' breakfast, when she heard a little noise outside. She opened the door, and there, within twenty-five feet of her, were three big Kodiak bears. Two of them stood up on their hin' feet when she opened the door, while the other kept smellin' around for grub."

"Goodness, Nina!" I exclaimed. "What was your first thought when you saw the big brutes so close?"

"Well," she answered, smiling, "my first thought was, 'What beautiful rugs those are on the backs of the bears! I want those rugs.'"

"Yes," Joe went on, "and so she stepped slowly back, inch by inch into the house, and softly closed the door so as not to *scare* the bears—they as big as a house and her such a leetle mite of a thing. She took down that 30-40 Winchester, there, and filled the magazine full (it chambers ten); and then she done a plumb foolish thing. I know darned well what I'd 'a' done. I'd 'a' poked the moss out between the logs, there, and stuck my rifle through and had some 'vantage."

"What did Nina do?" I asked.

"Why, she threw the door wide open and stepped right out in front of it. Up came all three bears, this time, on their hind feet. Nina's lightnin' on the snap shot, and before the big he-bear was straightened up he got it right between the eyes. Down he tumbled, and the other two was out of sight around the kennel there before she could throw another shell into the gun and aim." Joe pointed to a log dog-house about two rods in front of the door.

"Nina raced pell-mell past the kennel to get another shot, and there she saw the big she-bear, standin' up behind the dog-house, awaitin' for her, not a gun's length away. Nina swung around and fired pointblank into the bear's breast. It went down on all-fours and came for her with open mouth. There was nothing for it but to keep on shootin'. She worked the lever of her gun mighty fast. She put five bullets into the beast before she quieted it. She never saw the third bear again."

"Why, Nina!" I cried, as soon as I could get my breath. "You foolish child! Your escape was miraculous! It frightens me to hear Joe tell of it. Weren't you dreadfully scared when you saw that great brute jump at you like that?"

"Oh, no," laughed the girl. "I was too busy to get scared. But I was awfully provoked because the other one got away."

Other details of Nina's great adventure followed—how it took her three days to skin the two bears, she having to climb a tree to adjust the block and tackle so as to move the heavy carcases; and how Joe "blubbered" when he got home and saw them, and knew the peril his beloved had encountered.

Nina is an exceptional woman, but still she is truly a type. There is something in "that great, big, broad land, way up yonder," that stiffens the moral fiber, enlarges the spirit and makes the people unafraid. The white settlers of Alaska, while by no means all saints, are as a class the strongest, bravest and most resourceful people I know. I have not heard from my brave little chum for several years. I presume she is still living her joyous, fearless, Christian life in what John Muir used to call my "beautiful, fruitful wilderness." Here's to her; God bless her!

VIII

THE ABSURD WALRUS

Lewis Caroll's famous lines about the Walrus and the Carpenter will always hold their place at the very top of humorous poems. For besides being funny they have a quality of truth which the careless reader little suspects:

> "The time has come," the walrus said,
> "To talk of many things,
> Of shoes and ships and sealing wax,
> Of cabbages and kings;
> And why the sea is boiling hot,
> And whether pigs have wings."

The very few men who have been acquainted with the walrus in his native haunts know that the author of "Alice in Wonderland" in these verses "hits the nail on the head," and, perhaps unwittingly, gives an insight into the true character of the walrus as the most inconsistent, grotesque and absurd of all beasts.

It was my good fortune the summer of 1913 to be one of a company of six hunters on board the three-masted power schooner, *P. J. Abler*, which sailed along the Alaskan and Siberian coasts for six thousand miles and pounded its way northward into the Arctic ice-pack to within sixteen degrees of the Pole.

The ship itself was of unusual pattern. Her owner called her the *Mudhen*. Her three masts stood stiff and straight in a row and were the same height. Her lines were not particularly elegant, and her small engine could only push her through calm seas at the rate of five miles an hour. But she was a comfortable ship and had one quality in particular which overbalanced all the drawbacks and made her the boat for us—she was built for "bucking ice." She had extra heavy timbers, especially about her bow. In spite of her slowness, she was an ideal craft for venturing into Arctic ice-floes. She would come at a good speed, bow on, against a huge berg and bring up with a jar that would shake her as a rat shaken by a terrier, and send your plate of polar bear meat into your lap. Then she would recover from her backward bounce and calmly proceed on her way undented and unharmed. Mr. Scull of Philadelphia, who has sailed the world over, could never get used to bumping the ice. He and I would be bent over the chess board, absorbed in a difficult situation, when— bang! would go the schooner against the ice, and recoil, trembling like a hound. I would grab for the tottering chessmen, while Scull would jump right into the air with his hair standing straight up on each side of his bald pate like the ears of a horned owl. He would rush frantically out of the cabin door, lean far over the vessel's side, train his big eye-glasses on the ship's bow and watch for signs of her filling. Then he would come back muttering strange words in any of the five or six languages of which he is the master, and resume his study of the game, only to repeat the performance at the next bump. "Oh!" he would say, "it hurts me more than it hurts the ship"; which was undoubtedly true. I always had better luck in chess with Scull when we were bucking ice.

The personnel of our party was like some landscapes, varied and interesting. The commander of the expedition and its manager, was Captain Kleinschmidt, sailor, miner, hunter, author and moving-picture man. He chartered the *Abler* and hired her crew, who were as cosmopolitan as it is possible for crew to be—the captain, a Swede; the mate, a Dane; the engineers (brothers) German-Americans; the cook, a "Jap"; the crew composed of one American, one Russian and five Eskimos. There were two taxidermists to take care of the birdskins, bugs, mammals, etc., collected.

Of the four hunters, who, with Captain Kleinschmidt, financed the expedition, three were from Philadelphia: Scull, our polyglot interpreter, a publisher of books; Collins, a manufacturer; and Lovering, a young man who had lived part of his life in Wyoming. The fourth, Dr. Elting, was a surgeon of reputation from Albany, N. Y. All were experienced hunters, Scull and Collins having followed trails in Africa and America, Dr. Elting in the Western States and Canada, and Lovering in the West. As for myself, the guest without responsibility or care, "taken along," as the captain said, "to lend dignity to the expedition," you can call me by my common names: "The Sour-dough Preacher," "The Mushing Parson," "The Alaska Sky-Pilot," or any of half a dozen Northwestern cognomens, of all of which I am equally proud.

My object in joining this expedition was, first, to have a big hunt and a grand rest. But, more than the outing, I valued the privilege of exploring ground untrodden by the missionary, and, if possible, doing something towards bringing the Gospel to the heathen Eskimo of the Alaskan and Siberian shores.

We were all "out for a lark," glad beyond expression to be hundreds of miles from a telegram or newspaper, to be able to wear our dirty clothes and eat in our shirtsleeves without shame; to forget that such things existed as automobiles or stiff collars or dinner parties. We had four months of a royal good time—along the Asiatic Coast after Siberian sheep, on the Alaska Peninsula for caribou and brown bears, on Kenai Peninsula after moose, white sheep and black bear, among the islands of the Southern Alaska Coast and

Bering Sea with the bird and seal rookeries, and pursuing polar bear amid the ice-floes of the Arctic Ocean.

We visited many Eskimo villages; we shot for the museums hundreds of varieties of birds on the Siberian and Alaskan Coasts; we captured new species of beetles, moths, butterflies and other insects; the camera fiends and moving-picture man reveled in novel scenes, animate and inanimate. We buffeted storms, pounded ice and sailed sunny seas.

But the climax of our joyous outing was the three or four days we spent among the walrus herds off the Northern Siberian Coast. Scull and Collins, who had hunted everything in Africa from dikdik to rhinoceros, declared that none of their experiences in that continent approached in thrilling interest their days with the walrus herds.

For the walrus is *sui generis*: there is no other mammal at all like him in appearance, habits, habitat or characteristics. He is the least known or written about of all the larger animals. No thorough study has ever been made of him. More is known of the habits of the extinct woolly elephant—the mammoth, whose bones, tusks, and even hair and skin we find on the Alaskan Coast—than the walrus. And what has been written and the common ideas concerning this animal are so erroneous as to be funny.

A century or so ago a naturalist-traveler, writing about the Eskimos and the *morse*, as the walrus was then called, said that the tusks of the animal are for the purpose of pulling himself up the icy mountains where he lives; that his habit is to thus work his way up to the top of the dizziest peak; that the Eskimos pursue him there and cut holes through the thick skin of his flippers unknown to the huge pachyderm, whose hide is impervious to sensation. Then, having passed strong ropes through these holes and tied them to the jutting crags, they raise a hullabaloo, and the walrus, alarmed, precipitating himself down the mountain, jerks off his skin, which the Eskimos then use in the construction of their boats and houses. The year before our hunt, a California gentleman, interested in Captain K.'s moving pictures, asked him whether the walrus brought forth their young alive or laid eggs and hatched them.

In May, 1913, when discussing my proposed outing with some of my ministerial brethren, at the General Assembly at Atlanta, a good Doctor of Divinity tried to deter me from undertaking it because of its dangerous character.

"Is it not true, Dr. Young," he asked with great solicitude, "that the walrus sometimes devours human flesh?"

I patiently explained that the walrus has no incisors, no teeth at all but flat grinders, level with the gums and far back in the jaws, "and therefore he cannot rend or eat anything so very tough as a missionary"; and that moreover his mouth is situated back of a narrow opening of three or four inches in width between his tusks, so that nothing bulky can enter it. "He might drown me but he couldn't eat me!"

The "D. D." listened with open skepticism and put this poser: "How then can he devour his prey?"

"What prey?" I asked.

"Why, the seals and salmon and other large sea animals on which he feeds."

Again I sternly suppressed my rising emotions: "But he doesn't eat these things. He couldn't catch them and doesn't want them. He is only a clam- eater. His tusks are not spears, but an admirably constructed clam-hoe. He could not live without them; and his stiff whiskers form a fine brush to clean the clams of mud before he dines off them."

The good brother glanced from one to another of the listening group with a look that plainly said: "How sad it is that such shameless prevaricators will even slip into the ministry;" and walked off muttering something about consulting "authorities."

Illustrating my own roving habits, while a pioneer missionary in Alaska, I have sometimes said, using a common simile, that I "had no more home than a jack-rabbit." I am changing this now to a stronger expression; "no more home than a walrus." He is the most constantly on the move of all the vagabonds. Even when sleeping he is moving, for the only home the poor fellow has is the ice-cakes which form in the Arctic Ocean and Bering Sea, entirely filling the former and in the winter crowding down the latter to about fifty-eight degrees, north latitude. The walrus herds, for the greater part of the year, keep on the borders of this great field of ice. In the summer when the Bering Sea ice melts and also that of the southern part of the Arctic Ocean, the walrus keeps on the flat ice-cakes which float over the great clam beds of these shallow seas. As the ice forms in the fall and the ice-floes extend southward he sets out on a long swim ahead of the fast freezing ice, resting occasionally on the Siberian shore, the Diomedes, St. Lawrence, St. Matthews and other islands. When the ice-field has extended to its southern limit he resumes his ice-house-boat habit and returns north in the spring.

So little is known of the life history of the walrus that I am unable to speak with confidence, but the young are evidently brought forth very early in the spring, April or May, and float with their mothers (the females and young herding together), up into the Arctic Ocean as far as the shoals off Wrangle Island, one hundred and fifty miles north of the Siberian Coast. There the little ones are guarded by the cows, which during the summer months are the only really dangerous walrus ever met with. Were the walrus the ferocious and combatant animal he is sometimes depicted, it would be a risky thing indeed to hunt him in skin boats or any other small craft. Imagine three or four tons of muscular fierceness, armed with strong, sharp, spearlike tusks, charging at you. The front part of his head is a solid mass of tough bone more than a foot thick. He could strike his tusks through your boat and sink it in an instant, or hook them over the edge and upset you, spearing you one by one in the water.

But the huge pachyderm is the most timid and good-natured of animals. It is only when the female fears for the safety of her young that she shows anything like ferocity. In 1911 Captain Kleinschmidt was taking moving pictures of the walrus herds. He had two catamarans, made by lashing two kyaks together with firm cross pieces. In the foremost craft two Eskimo hunters with their spears were paddling ahead, to slip up on the herds and harpoon them at the proper time, while the moving-picture man was in the other craft to take pictures of the herds and of the whole performance.

A herd of cows and their young had been frightened from an ice-cake into the water. Suddenly one of these cows thrust her tusks forward, the sign of a charge: "Look out!" cried K. to the Eskimo as the cow dived. They made frantic efforts to paddle their kyaks to the nearest berg, but the cow came up under the craft and slashed with her tusks one of the kyaks, ripping the bottom and filling it with water. The other kyak of the catamaran tilted dangerously, the Eskimo in the sinking one throwing himself upon it, and the two frightened natives made their escape to the ice-cake. Coming to the surface again the cow sighted Captain K.'s catamaran, thrust her tusks forward again and dived; he saw her body deep in the water coming toward him and thought his time had come; but luckily when she struck the canoe had veered and received only a glancing blow. She came to the surface within a yard of the picture man, who had his rifle ready and thrust it against her brain and pulled the trigger, which ended that affair. But it was a perilous adventure, and one is liable to meet with such if he is so rash as to venture among the herds of the cows with their young.

During this hunt of ours, although we saw great herds aggregating hundreds of walrus, we did not see a cow or calf among them; only the big bulls herded together and occasionally a solitary one.

After passing Cape Prince of Wales into the Arctic Ocean we had a week of battling with winds and tide before we got into the ice-pack well up towards Wrangell and Herald Islands. We had another week of pounding ice, poking through the narrow "leads," constantly turning and running the other way in our effort to get to the shores where the walrus herds would feed.

We had fun with the polar bears, but, with one exception, saw no walrus for nearly two weeks of this strenuous fight. This one exception was a big old bull that we sighted reposing in solitary dignity on an ice-cake in the midst of this vast white solitude.

Captain K. took Dr. Elting with him in the kyaks which we manufactured into a catamaran, and while the *Abler* lay "off and on" the two hunters whom we watched through our field-glasses made their sinuous way behind ice hummocks through the narrow "leads" and around the jamming cakes of the ice-field. We saw them at last seemingly right upon the walrus, on the same cake. The big fellow was fast asleep in the uneasy fashion that all walrus and seal have of sleeping; that is, every two or three minutes they will raise their heads and move them back and forth, during which time the hunters must keep perfectly still and if possible behind the ice-cakes. The walrus, however, has not the keen sight of the seal, and is more easily approached.

Our hunters moored their skin boat on the ice-cake close to the walrus, crept up behind a hummock right upon him, and Dr. Elting put his bullet into the brain of the beast, which is situated in his neck, and not in what appears to be his head. It was an easy and not very exciting triumph. What possessed this old bull to lie there alone scores of miles from his companions, I do not know. He may have been there two or three weeks on that one ice-cake, as the Eskimos tell us this is sometimes their habit.

It was not until August eighteenth that we got sight of our first walrus herd, and then for three days we were right in the midst of them. We had been driven by buffeting winds and threatening ice-packs away from the vicinity of the islands far westward along the Siberian coast and were perhaps thirty or forty miles from land. The cry was raised from the "crow's nest": "Walrus!"

The appearance of the herd as we approached it was very unlike anything imagined by those who had not hitherto seen these animals. All sorts of comparisons crowd upon one's imagination when trying to describe them. Some of them look like huge caterpillars and have an exactly similar motion, except that their antennæ are bent downward instead of upward. Sometimes when bunched up they look like immense squirrels. Sometimes when scratching themselves with their flippers they have the languid movements of a fashionable lady fanning herself; and again, when two are sparring at each other, they have the fierce mien of gladiators. But always there is that particularly comical edge about them that impels to irresistible laughter, as when one approaches a cage of monkeys. Their attitudes and motions are so unexpected and ridiculous.

I did little hunting myself but went with the other hunters in the *oomiak* or large skin boat; and I believe I got more enjoyment than any one else of the party; for I was not doing the killing, and was enjoying equally the misses and the hits of the others and, above all, the study of these huge and interesting brutes. Many of my preconceived notions, obtained by reading and by hearsay, were put to flight during those three or four days.

Only a few years ago a report to the Smithsonian Institute was published in which it was stated that the walrus were very watchful and wary, and that when reposing on the ice-cake they selected a large bull to climb the highest pinnacle and keep watch for foes, and that when he grew weary of his vigil and wished to sleep he would prod the bull next to him with his tusks and let him take his turn while the former watchman took a nap. It was thus inferred that the walrus scanned the region of ice with eagle eyes and had a system of signalling similar to the organized human gunboats or armies.

But this is all nonsense. The fact is that the walrus cannot see more than ten or twelve feet at the most, and even at that distance I doubt whether he can distinguish more than the mere outlines of any object. His eyes are the eyes of a fish, small and rudely constructed and exceptionally nearsighted. They are made for use in the dim depths of the sea. When the sun shines the walrus shut their eyes and apparently cannot open them. When alarmed they rush into the water and then come up and will crowd within five or six feet of the moving-picture man or hunter, bulging their eyes like those of a crab in frantic attempts to see their foe.

We clad ourselves in white muslin parkas, and got our *oomiaks* or *kyaks* boldly up under the noses of these great beasts with them staring down upon us. The only thing we had to guard against was their getting our wind. If we kept to leeward of them we were always out of their sight. The strange bulging of the eyes when excited gives a most grotesque appearance to the countenance of these walrus, as ordinarily their eyes are deep sunken in their heads.

Let me sketch a picture from life: It is the twentieth of August. We are in the vicinity of Cape North on the Northern Siberian coast. We are twenty or thirty miles offshore. The day is warm, sunny, still. The ship is tied to a large iceberg; a wilderness of floating ice-cakes stretches in every direction to the horizon. In some places these are massed together; again there will be little open places, and ragged leads, but everywhere ice, ice, ice. And it is all in motion; a slow heaving and grinding of the floe, and the tidal currents moving in different directions and with varied rapidity, but all trending northwest, the landscape—or seascape—changing every minute. There are herds of walrus all around us, some numerous, containing two or three hundred on one cake of ice, others small; here a group of four or five big bulls on a cake just large enough to hold them; then fifteen or twenty on a wider berg with little hummocks, up the slopes of which the big brutes crowd.

Scull and Lovering have taken the kyak-catamaran and are paddling to the nearest bunch of walrus not five hundred yards from the ship. Captain K. has launched the big skin boat, or *oomiak*, and is perched on the high stern, steering. His aeroscope moving-picture machine and graphlex camera, his field-glass and rifle are by him. "Eskimo Prank" and I are in front of him with our paddles; while Dr. Elting and Collins are in the bow, with paddles in their hands and their big Ross and Mannlicher rifles close by. We corkscrew our way through the ice, steering past a bunch of walrus on a small cake. "Small ice—lose um quick," says Prank. We are heading to a herd of twenty or thirty, with some big tuskers among them. We keep to the leeward of them, for the sense of smell seems to be their one keen sense, and even that does not compare in acuteness with the nose of the polar bear or the caribou.

Captain K. and "Eskimo Prank" are the only ones in our party who are perfectly calm and unexcited, and they seem to the rest of us rash and careless. The boat is steered right in sight of the herd, and we are getting close to them. Now the big, ugly heads of five or six which have been digging clams come up right alongside of us. Suddenly their heads rise high out of the water and their sunken eyes bulge out as they stare up into our faces. It takes a whole minute's scrutiny to satisfy them that we are enemies, and they go down with great splashing and blowing to come up again almost in the same place and stare at us again. So we are escorted up to the edge of the ice-cake on which the herd reposes. As a precaution against discovery we list the *oomiak* so that its side protects us from their sight.

We range alongside the cake; "Prank" and I hold it steady by clutching spurs of ice. The captain with his picture machines, and the hunters with their guns crawl out on the ice. They are clad in white parkas—but there is plenty to see about them in all conscience, and they make plenty of noise. We are only twenty or thirty feet from the nearest walrus. Two or three big bulls are on the hummock right above us. The captain and the hunters maneuver about, cautiously but sometimes in plain sight, and discuss, in voices clearly audible three times the distance, the question as to which have the best tusks, which lie most favorably for a good shot, in which hump of the neck the brain lies and just where to shoot. The captain gets his bulky aeroscope placed and sets the engine to buzzing and clacking. The hunters are waiting for the beasts to turn just right so as to expose the brain. For the brain of a walrus is as small as that of a rhinoceros in proportion to its size—about as big as one's two fists, —and you must know just where it is, and place your ball right through it, or your game will flop and flounder in his dying struggles and roll into the sea and you'll lose him. Hence the nervous care and uncertainty of the hunters. For ten or fifteen minutes we wait for the chance, the favorable moment.

But about that foolish sentinel story: A beast that cannot tell an *oomiak* full of bipeds, or these same bipeds with guns or cameras from a fellow walrus at the distance of ten yards, doesn't plan and place a relay of watchmen. We learned from close and long observation that the walrus couldn't see us in the sunshine—their eyes were shut, or nearly so, and dim when open. Neither can they hear well. They have no external ear at all, only a tiny hole which requires close observation to discover. Even the near roar of a heavy rifle does not always alarm them, and hunters with smaller rifles have killed one after another of a whole herd until all were slain, without causing a stampede. Of course the repeated shots of two or three rifles close at hand will generally cause them to rush into the water, but even that does not always scare them. A heavy shot near by will bring all heads up, but if it is not repeated they will soon go to sleep again.

But what a thrilling time it was for me as I sat in the boat or on the ice-cake and watched the drama! It was far more comedy than tragedy. The great beasts, as heavy as elephants, were lying in bunches or rolling around like a lot of huge, fat hogs. Here a great bull with long tusks was lying on his back and scratching himself against an ice hummock, wriggling and squirming like a Newfoundland dog. Another was curled up in an impossible heap and scratching the top of his head with his hind flipper. Another was making his way through a bunch of sleeping comrades, rolling them around or scrambling over them and fighting those that resented his intrusion. Some were swimming about the landing place of low ice and trying to scramble onto the cake, and these would disturb a whole bunch of the lazy animals and there would be trouble.

And the noises they made were as various and interesting as their positions. One huge fellow, so close to me that I could have punched him with a bamboo fishing-rod, shook his head slowly from side to side with shut eyes and groaned with a dismal falling cadence, for all the world like a fat old man with the rheumatism: "O-o-o-h: D-e-a-r me, d-e-a-r me; this world's a wilderness of woe!"

Another was optimistic, and his was a sigh of infinite content. "A-a-h-h!" he said, "what a nice, soft, warm bed this ice-cake is! How fat and delicious those clams were! And I don't believe there is one of those horrible, malodorous little human bipeds with his deadly bang-stick within a hundred miles of us." And there we were within twenty feet of him, trying to locate his brain-pan!

Some grunted like pigs in sheer laziness. Others barked sharply as they prodded each other with their strong, sharp tusks: "Get off my stomach, you lazy son of a clam-digger! Wow! Wow!"

Two of them were sparring like gladiators, raising their heads high and roaring defiance; but it was all good nature, for in a minute they were lying asleep, one with his head across the other's neck.

All their movements, attitudes and voices had such a droll element; all were so irresistibly funny that I wanted to lie down on my back and roar with laughter.

But our hunters wanted big heads and tusks as trophies; our Eskimos desired some hides to make their *oomiaks* and to cover their houses; and we wanted tons of meat for the women and children of the Siberian villages. And so after a while the rifles roared and roared again and again, and the hunters moved close up, working their levers fast. The mad scramble of the walrus for the water was a most grotesque sight. They charged blindly ahead whichever way they happened to be lying, humping up their backs as they drew their hind flippers under them and stretching out again, just like the "woolly bear" caterpillars I used to tease when a boy. Those that escaped the volley splashed heavily into the water and dived deep, but presently they were all at the surface again, blowing and coughing, bunching in masses, crowding close to the feet of the moving-picture man, stretching their heads six feet out of the water, popping and rolling their ochre-colored eyes in frantic efforts to see. Then one would get a whiff of the dreaded man-scent and would go down with a mighty splash and snort, and the whole crowd would follow suit, soon to come up and repeat the performance five or six times before they could finally get it into their slow brains that this was a dangerous neighborhood.

We had four most interesting days among the walrus, and the hunters were sated with sport and trophies. My wishes were more modest. I had announced to Dr. John Timothy Stone, the Moderator of the Atlanta General Assembly, 1913, that my grand object in going on this hunt was to kill a walrus myself, get his tusks and have a couple of ivory gavels made out of them, that I might present them to the outgoing and incoming moderators of the next General Assembly, which was to meet in Chicago, 1914.

I got my walrus in this fashion: Captain K., Dr. Elting and I were in the *oomiak* with "Eskimo Prank." Dr. E. had got a fine head, and we were cruising about, when we spied a bunch of seven or eight big walrus on a hummocky berg near the edge of the ice-floe. The swell of the open ocean came in here with considerable force, and long, smooth topped billows heaved among the ice-floes, washing far up on the shelving bergs. We pushed our boat into a narrow passage and the swell took it and landed the bow on the ice right in the midst of the walrus. The captain and the doctor took the hazardous chance and leaped on the ice, placing the muzzles of their rifles almost against the heads of their selection. I was not quick enough to make the jump, but as the *oomiak* surged back with the receding wave I saw a walrus charging down the sloping ice diagonally from me. Both he and I were moving rapidly and in opposite directions and I could only take a hasty "wing" shot. It was the most difficult shot of all my experience. I was standing uncertainly in the plunging *oomiak*, swaying and tottering as the light craft shot down the receding wave away from the iceberg; while the frightened walrus was humping himself for all he was worth, trying frantically to get off the ice-floe into the ocean, his head bobbing up and down with his rapid motion. I was wobbling in one direction and he in another, and the space between us was widening fast. There was no time to be lost. Balancing most unsteadily, I swung up my rifle for a snap shot. It was a great moment. I had little hope of hitting the mark; but my walrus fell to the crack of the rifle, with his nose in the water. A delay of one-tenth of a second and I would have lost him. I had my gavels.

The closing scene of our walrus drama was a comedy scene, and possessed what every drama ought to have—human interest. We had pounded our way southeast again through the fast thickening ice-floe driven upon us by a strong northwest wind. At one time to the least experienced of the party it seemed as if there was no possible way out, as if we must spend the winter on the bleak shore of Northern Siberia. But always the narrow leads opened before us, and after two or three days of slow and careful work through the ice we emerged from it, and before a strong, fair wind we bowled along towards Bering Strait. The early morning of August twenty-fifth found us anchored in the harbor of East Cape, after a hard struggle against wind and tide.

Here is a large Eskimo village. The Tchukchees, or reindeer-herding Eskimos do not roam as far north as this, and these were the seal and walrus hunters. They depend almost entirely for their food upon the sea, and a shortage of these animals sometimes causes starvation.

This village is situated behind a high bluff, but it is not well sheltered, and a fierce wind offshore caused the ship to tug violently at her anchor, and made landing difficult. Captain K. and the Eskimos got a boat ashore and secured a stout line to the ship. Then the eight or nine great carcases on our deck were heaved by the donkey engine into the sea. They would float by this time. They were not spoiled at all in the estimation of the Eskimo, only "ripe." They were tied to the line and then a large crowd of Eskimos took hold, ran up the beach and so towed the meat ashore.

Then, what a scene! Out from every one of those large balloon-framed, skin-covered houses poured the men, women and children, shouting, screaming, hurrying in joy and excitement. The men with high waterproof mukluks were cutting up the carcases, and men and women would seize the hunks of meat and rush away to their houses, pursued by scores of wolfish dogs which leaped and snapped at the meat. Occasionally the dogs would succeed in getting away with a large chunk, when instantly there would be a general mix- up from which some of the dogs would emerge limping and howling. There was a dog-fight every five minutes.

The moving-picture man and the camera fiends moved about "taking" the crowd. The men with old ivory ornaments, white ivory implements, and other curios to sell besieged the white men. In all the houses cooking was going on, and many were chewing on the raw blubber. It was a day of days to these poor people, and for the first time on our voyage of pleasure we felt ourselves benefactors to the human race. "The calendar of these Eskimos will date from to-day," said the only American white man who lives in East Cape village. "They will count time all winter from the day of the big feed of walrus meat."

But better than the meat for their bodies which we procured for these poor people of the Arctic shore, was the Bread of Life that I was able to direct to several Eskimo towns, from the knowledge gained in this great walrus hunt.

Printed in the United States of America

www.ingramcontent.com/pod-product-compliance
Lightning Source LLC
Chambersburg PA
CBHW060801310726
48980CB00002B/180

* 9 7 8 3 7 3 2 6 2 0 4 9 4 *